Praise for the Inspector DeKok series by Baantjer

"Along with such peers as Ed McBain and Georges Simenon, [Baantjer] has created a long-running and uniformly engaging police series. They are smart, suspenseful, and better-crafted than most in the field."
—*Mystery Scene*

"Baantjer's laconic, rapid-fire storytelling has spun out a surprisingly complex web of mysteries."
—*Kirkus Reviews*

"DeKok is a careful, compassionate policeman in the tradition of Maigret; crime fans will enjoy this book."
—*Library Journal*

"DeKok's maverick personality certainly makes him a compassionate judge of other outsiders and an astute analyst of antisocial behavior."
—*The New York Times Book Review*

"It's easy to understand the appeal of Amsterdam police detective DeKok; he hides his intelligence behind a phlegmatic demeanor, like an old dog that lazes by the fireplace and only shows his teeth when the house is threatened."
—*The Los Angeles Times*

Inspector DeKok Series

Titles Available or Forthcoming from Speck Press

DeKok AND
Murder on Blood Mountain

Number 23 in the Inspector DeKok Series

by
A. C. Baantjer

Translated by H. G. Smittenaar

speck press
denver

Published by *Speck Press,* speckpress.com
An imprint of Fulcrum Publishing
Printed and bound in the United States of America
ISBN: 1-933108-13-4, ISBN13: 978-1-933108-13-1
Book layout and design by: Margaret McCullough, corvusdesignstudio.com

English translation by H. G. Smittenaar copyright © 2007 Speck Press.
Translated from *De Cock en moord op de Bloedberg,* by Baantjer (Albert Cornelis
Baantjer), copyright © 1985 by Uitgeverij De Fontein bv, Baarn, Netherlands.

Library of Congress Cataloging-in-Publication Data
Baantjer, A. C.
[De Cock en moord op de Bloedberg. English]
DeKok and murder on Blood Mountain / by A.C. Baantjer ; translated by H.G.
Smittenaar.
p. cm. -- (Inspector Dekok series ; no. 23)
ISBN-13: 978-1-933108-13-1 (pbk. : alk. paper)
ISBN-10: 1-933108-13-4 (pbk. : alk. paper)
I. Title.

PT5881.12.A2D57713 2007
839.3'1364--dc22

2007028179

10 9 8 7 6 5 4 3 2 1

1

An icy polar wind came down from an overcast sky and raced along the frozen Amstel River. It chased unopposed through the bare branches of the trees and bushes. It even seemed to shrink the eternal green of the majestic conifers on either side of the gate.

Shivering, slightly hunched, Inspector DeKok walked along the wide entrance path to Sorrow Field Cemetery.

The gravel crunched under his feet as his weight broke the small icy cocoons encasing the stones. He could no longer feel his ears and, with an impatient gesture, he pulled up the wide collar of his winter coat. He pushed his old, decrepit little hat farther down over his forehead. He wondered idly how anyone was able to dig a grave in this Siberian cold. The ground must be permafrost.

He turned his head slightly and looked at Vledder, his partner, friend, and assistant.

"I think the frost is down deep in the ground."

The younger inspector shrugged his shoulders as he pointed at the gravestones surrounding them.

"You're afraid they're getting cold?"

It sounded callous and cynical.

DeKok gave him a chastening look.

"That's inappropriate," he reprimanded.

Vledder hugged himself in an effort to get a little warmer.

"I don't know about you," he said with nearly chattering teeth, "but if I were to die now, at this moment, I'd ask for a spot in Hell. As far as I know, it's always warm there."

The gray sleuth did not appreciate the profane joke. His puritan soul, formed by his Calvinistic upbringing, rebelled at the thought. Dying and the possibility of life after death were, he felt, mysteries that should not be the object of levity.

"There will be groaning and weeping and the gnashing of teeth."

"Where?"

"In Hell."

With a grin, Vledder abandoned the subject.

"Why are we actually here, in this icebox?"

"To attend a funeral."

"Whose funeral?"

"The deceased is a certain Henry Assumburg."

"Are we supposed to know him?"

DeKok looked serious.

"Hendrik-Jan Assumburg, to use his full name, is a Dutch citizen who died in Belgium."

"How?"

"He was murdered."

The younger inspector was surprised.

"Murdered?" he repeated.

DeKok nodded.

"They fished him out of the harbor, near one of their docks."

"Drowned?"

"No, poisoned. The Belgian investigating judge ordered an autopsy. The coroner found no water in the lungs and concluded he was dead before he hit the water."

Vledder shrugged his shoulders.

"We have nothing to do with a murder in Belgium."

DeKok shook his head.

"We don't. We're here at the request of the Antwerp police."

"To do what?"

DeKok did not answer immediately. He looked at a group of people who leaned against the lee wall of the chapel, trying to escape the sharp, cold wind.

An ageing undertaker, dressed in morning clothes complete with tails and high hat, shivered as he presented the condolence register to the mourners. As he stepped out of the lee of the chapel, the wind tore the hat off his head and chased it across the frozen ground among the gravestones.

DeKok ran after the hat as somebody along the wall laughed. DeKok at top speed was a comical sight.

The hat caught in the fence around a white marble monument. DeKok grabbed the hat and ambled back. The undertaker walked toward him.

With a friendly smile, DeKok returned the man's hat.

"My name is DeKok," he said softly, "with a kay-oh-kay." He pointed at Vledder. "That is my colleague. We're inspectors attached to Warmoes Street station."

The undertaker looked puzzled.

"Police?"

DeKok nodded.

"I have a small, but confidential, request."

"And what might that be?"

"Will you make sure," answered DeKok, almost whispering, "that all interested parties sign the condolence register? And ask if they will also print their names next to the signatures. The signatures are usually unreadable."

The undertaker nodded his understanding.

"And then you want the register?"

DeKok smiled.

"Privately, you understand? I don't want anybody else to know. I'll borrow it for just a few hours…not longer. Then you'll get it back undamaged and will be able to present it to the family."

They walked back together.

"There will be a small ceremony in the chapel. Will you attend?"

"Certainly."

A long, gleaming hearse approached across the gravel. The procession of cars stopped a little distance away. The doors of the chapel opened and the pallbearers lifted the flower-covered coffin from the hearse.

With his head bared, DeKok watched and silently prayed his ears would not freeze off in the bitter cold.

DeKok had always admired the efficient way in which services for the dead were conducted in Holland. The nondenominational chapel on the cemetery grounds had two large doors at either end. As one funeral party departed through a set of doors, the next funeral party would enter through the other doors. A brief service was held, and the cycle repeated itself. Few families elected to have funeral services in their own churches.

Following the procession of mourners, DeKok and Vledder entered the chapel and took their place at the back wall. As they leaned against the oaken wainscotting, they watched a man in a dark suit walk to the dais and arrange some papers in front of him.

The man looked around the chapel, coughed discreetly, and then raised his arms in a theatrical gesture.

"*May God*," he thundered, "*give you His blessings and peace. Amen.*" He lowered his arms and continued in a more moderate tone of voice. "And Jesus said, 'I am the resurrection and the life; he that believeth in me, though he were dead, yet shall he live. And whoever liveth and believeth in me shall never die.' Today we take leave of…"

DeKok allowed the preacher's words to pass over him as he observed the backs of the gathering. Near the front was a young woman, veiled and dressed in black. He figured she was around thirty years of age. Next to her was a dignified man with just a hint of gray hair at the temples. From time to time he glanced sideways at the woman.

Suddenly DeKok's attention reverted back to the speaker. The speaker was gesticulating energetically.

"*De mortuis nil nisi bene*," he exclaimed with relish. "Of the dead…of the dead you will hear me speak no evil. We mortals have not the right to judge his deeds. If his life, by whatever measure, was wrongly lived, he will already have been judged by Him who is all knowing. We do not know, and will probably never learn these facts." The speaker fell silent for a moment and then leaned forward. After a long look at the audience, he bowed his head. "Let us pray for mercy for the killer."

After a fiery prayer, heavy organ music descended on the mourners. The preacher left the dais. The professional pallbearers arranged themselves around the coffin and then carried the coffin outside.

Vledder and DeKok followed slowly at a distance. It was still bitterly cold, but the wind had died down a little. The temperature seemed just that much more bearable.

DeKok punched his hat more or less into its original shape and allowed the distance between them and the mourners to increase slightly. Vledder matched his pace.

"I still don't know what we're doing here."

DeKok pointed in the direction of the coffin.

"At the request of the Antwerp police, we are discreetly attending the funeral."

The young inspector grinned.

"You can hardly call the way you ran after the undertaker's hat as 'discreet attendance.'"

DeKok smiled sourly as he looked aside.

"Don't you think the preacher's sermon was bit strange? I'll have to digest his words some more, but it seems to me his intentions were to say something specific to one of the attendees."

Vledder nodded.

"Trying to say what and to whom?"

DeKok shrugged.

"That's hard to say. Either the man spoke about his own experiences, knew the murderer, or somebody whispered something in his ear." He nodded to himself.

"It might not be a bad idea to ask the man some pointed questions."

"Why?" Vledder asked, annoyed. "What business is it of ours? The request of the Antwerp police was to attend the funeral. So let's leave well enough alone. It's a Belgian murder. We certainly have enough on our plates at Warmoes Street."

DeKok walked on, deep in thought.

"It's just too bad we know nothing at all about Henry Assumburg."

"Personally, I don't *want* to know anything about him. Let's keep it that way."

DeKok ignored the remark.

"'If his life was wrongly lived, by whatever measure, he will already have been judged by Him who is all knowing.' Those were the exact words of the preacher." DeKok pushed his lower lip out, which gave him a belligerent expression. He pointed at the coffin. "It seems that the man in the coffin did not exactly lead an exemplary life. I wouldn't be at all surprised if his life choices lead us to the murderer's motive, and—"

Vledder interrupted.

"DeKok," he almost barked, "stop it. It is *not* our case. Leave it for our colleagues in Antwerp. They know what they're doing, I'm sure." He gave his older colleague a sarcastic look. "Or do you think they're waiting for help from DeKok...with a kay-oh-kay?"

The gray sleuth rubbed his chin. He understood Vledder better than anybody. The case of the "golf club" murders had just been concluded, and they could still feel the exhaustion of nightly excursions in their bones.

The procession reached the gravesite. DeKok took off his hat and joined the circle. The preacher had re-appeared and began to speak.

"It has pleased almighty God," he orated, "to call our brother Hendrik-Jan Assumburg…with a firm belief in the resurrection, we now place his body in the grave…earth to earth, ashes to ashes, dust to dust…"

DeKok absorbed the words only vaguely. His focus was directed at the circle of mourners.

The young, veiled woman was beautiful, he noticed. The distinguished gentleman with the gray at the temples supported her. The way he did it irritated DeKok. It was too insistent, too demonstrative; it was not a sign of real compassion or grief. Besides, the young woman did not look as if she needed to be supported.

Letting his eyes move through the crowd, DeKok abruptly noticed a face in the outer circle across from him. It was a narrow, white face. For just a moment their eyes met in mutual recognition.

DeKok gasped with surprise. His legs seemed to be rooted to the ground, unable to move for a few minutes. Then, breaking free from his paralysis, he worked his way between the people behind him and circled toward the place where he had seen the face. He was too late. When he arrived at the spot, he saw a man about a hundred feet away, running toward the cemetery exit with his coat whipping in the wind.

Wildly, DeKok ran in pursuit. At first it seemed he was gaining slightly, but the distance between the two became greater. After a few hundred feet, DeKok gave in. Breathing heavily he sank down on a bench under a bald weeping willow. He undid the top button of his shirt, despite the chilled air.

Vledder arrived at a run, red in the face with exertion.

"What...what," he stammered, "do you think you're doing? It's outrageous. You disrupted the ceremony."

Slowly DeKok regained his breath.

"I ran after a man."

"What sort of man?"

"Ronald Kruisberg."

Vledder looked a question.

"No, I meant, is he a fugitive? Are we looking for him?"

DeKok shook his head.

"He died...two years ago."

2

Vledder used his sleeve to remove a dusting of snow from the windshield of the old VW Beetle. Then he entered the car, started the engine, and drove away. The wipers worked only at slow speed, and the heater was just barely able to defrost the windshield. The rest of the car was like an icebox.

DeKok sank down in the passenger seat. Despite the frigid temperature in the car, he was reasonably comfortable. He silently blessed his wife, who insisted he wear a hand-knit woolen sweater during any month with an "R" in the name.

He shook his head in disgust.

"Two sprints in the last forty-five minutes? I'm getting too old for this stuff."

Vledder shrugged.

"Why didn't you warn me? Maybe I could have caught him."

DeKok shrugged.

"What should I have done? I can't imagine calling out loud, 'There is a dead man standing about...go catch him!'" He snorted. "A remarkable exclamation for a funeral ceremony, don't you think?" He grinned boyishly. "Besides," he added, "my old mother would never have forgiven me for interrupting a minister during his sermon."

The young inspector laughed.

"Even so, you created enough of a disturbance. I don't think anybody heard the *Our Father.*"

"I'm sorry about that."

Vledder gave him a quick but penetrating look.

"Are you sure?" he asked.

"What?"

"Are you sure Ronald Kruisberg is dead?"

DeKok pressed himself more upright in the seat.

"Years ago, before your time, when there was no homicide squad at Warmoes Street, I was investigating a fraud case in which Kruisberg was a suspect. He had started a company and sold property in Spain for future vacation homes. When a few of his customers actually took a look in Spain, it turned out the parcels were situated in a remote region. The rough, rocky ground had not the remotest chance of access to water or any other utilities. In fact, there wasn't even a track, let alone a road, for access. The ground was worthless. He must have cheated hundreds of people."

"Did you solve the case?"

"Oh, yes," nodded DeKok. "I had a number of conversations with Kruisberg at the time. He was a friendly, pleasant man. But when I finally received permission from the judge advocate to make an arrest, Kruisberg had flown the coop."

Vledder nodded wisely.

"With all the money."

"Precisely."

"And why do—did—you think he's dead?"

DeKok took a deep breath.

"When he disappeared without a trace, I sent out an APB with a request to arrest him and deliver him to Amsterdam so we could charge him. Nothing turned up. Then, about two years ago, I read an obituary in the paper stating Ronald Kruisberg had been killed in a traffic accident in Belgium. I immediately contacted the registry office, and they confirmed he was registered as deceased."

It became clear to Vledder.

"And so you, of course, cancelled the APB."

"Yes, of course. It was of no use. Prosecution, it states in the law, is no longer possible after the death of the suspect."

Vledder stopped for a red light. He looked pensive. After the light turned green and he was through the intersection, he spoke again.

"There's no chance you made a mistake?"

DeKok seemed surprised at the question.

"You mean that the man at the cemetery was *not* Ronald Kruisberg?"

"Yes, perhaps you saw someone else, someone who resembles him. Could have been a brother..."

DeKok rubbed the back of his neck, deep in thought.

"No," he said after a long pause. "I have the distinct impression he recognized me as well. It's hard to make a mistake about that. Besides, if he isn't Ronald Kruisberg, why would he run away?"

Vledder smiled.

"If I saw you run at me, I'd flee, too."

DeKok laughed.

"Do you have a bad conscience?"

The young man shook his head.

"You've no idea how dangerous you can look."

DeKok ignored the remark. Instead he closed his eyes and allowed the scene at the cemetery to replay in his mind.

"I think," he said slowly, "that he started to run the moment he realized I had recognized him."

Vledder remained silent, a stubborn look on his face. He found it impossible to accept a man rising from the dead. For a while he concentrated on his driving.

"How long since you last saw Ronald Kruisberg alive?" he asked finally.

DeKok glanced at the clock on the dashboard.

"About half an hour ago."

"Don't be smart. I mean *before* that moment."

"About twelve years."

Vledder nodded pensively.

"A man can change his appearance a lot in twelve years' time."

DeKok rubbed his chin.

"Possibly, but expressions do not change so easily. They give an impression of the individual, a so-called *gestalt*. That's the way it is with our Ronald." He paused. "You know what I can't help wondering?"

"No."

"Why did he take the risk to attend Assumburg's funeral? Why chance being recognized?"

Vledder gave his partner a measured look. He felt

DeKok was becoming enamored of the idea that Kruisberg was still alive. If so, DeKok might be tempted to reopen the investigation, an investigation that had nothing to do with homicide. He made a dismissive gesture with one hand.

"What's all this talk about risk?" he asked, irritated. "Why don't you simply admit you made a mistake? That's nothing to be ashamed of—it's only human. It has happened to me, too. Several times I thought I had definitely seen someone, somewhere. But in retrospect it turned out to be a mistake."

DeKok shook his head.

"There's nothing wrong with my powers of observation," he said stubbornly.

Vledder sighed in exasperation.

"If Ronald Kruisberg is dead," he said patiently, "he's dead and therefore was *not* at the funeral. It's that simple."

DeKok shrugged.

"Dead or alive—he was there."

Vledder tried to stay calm. His annoyance was turning to anger.

"What utter nonsense."

The gray sleuth looked at his young partner. He recognized the symptoms of growing irritation.

"All right," he said soothingly. "You're right. It is nonsense…against all logic, I know that. Dead is dead, and death is irrevocable." But then he stuck out his chin and a determined look came into his eyes. He slapped a fist on the dashboard. "But I do *not* suffer from hallucinations. I saw a living Ronald Kruisberg. If Kruisberg has somehow cheated death, I have a long list of people in the bottom drawer of my desk whom he cheated out of hundreds of thousands of euros...although they were still guilders in those days," he added innocuously. He paused to take a deep breath. Then he continued, "And those people would like to know, even at this late date, what happened to their hard-earned savings."

Vledder leaned closer over the steering wheel and remained silent. He realized DeKok had the bit between his teeth and was determined to pursue the case.

There was less traffic in town, so he was making good progress. It seemed the brutal weather held people prisoner in their houses. That changed when he came close to the station house. A truck was unloading in the middle of the street, causing a long backup. Vledder put the gearshift in neutral and set the hand brake. He turned to face DeKok.

"If," he began carefully, "Ronald Kruisberg is still alive, who's in his grave?"

DeKok suddenly looked happier. He slapped his hands together.

"Dick," he said with genuine admiration, "that is a very intelligent question."

DeKok pushed his chair aside and knelt down behind his desk. He pulled open the bottom drawer. Vledder looked down on him from in front of the desk.

"What are you doing?"

DeKok looked up.

"I'm looking for the old files on Spanish Enterprises."

"Kruisberg's company?"

DeKok nodded, bending back to his task.

"I should have turned the files over to archives, but, for one reason or another, I just couldn't let go of them. I recall a loud conversation with the judge advocate because he was so slow to react. I *told* him the man was a flight risk…and, sure enough, Kruisberg ran."

Vledder nodded his understanding. DeKok had never, in his memory, backed away from speaking his mind. He was sure the "conversation" with the judge advocate would have been heated, to say the least.

"But isn't the case too old by now? Surely it must have lapsed after all this time?"

"As far as the criminal court is concerned, we can't prosecute Kruisberg for the fraud anymore. But civil actions are still possible."

Vledder grinned.

"But only if Kruisberg is still alive, and still has the money."

"Yes, there's that."

Adjutant Kamphuis entered the detective room and steered a course for DeKok's desk. He tossed a large gray envelope on the desk and then discovered DeKok on the floor behind the desk.

"An undertaker just delivered this for you," he said.

"Thanks."

Vledder looked curiously at the envelope.

"What's that?"

DeKok came slowly to his feet and opened the envelope.

"The condolence register from the Assumburg funeral

with, I hope, all the names of the interested parties in a legible form."

"You asked for that?"

DeKok smiled mischievously.

"You don't think I ran after the man's hat just for the fun of it, do you?" He handed the book to Vledder. "Make copies of all the pages. Two sets, one set for our colleagues in Antwerp, along with our report on the funeral."

"What should I say in the report?"

DeKok shrugged.

"'Assumburg buried without incident.'"

"That's all?"

"Yes."

"What about the original register?"

"Get it back to the undertaker as soon as possible. I only borrowed it for a little while. Then he can hand it to the family...along with his bill, no doubt."

Vledder sat down at his desk and leafed through the pages. Suddenly he looked up.

"He's here."

"Who?"

"The late Kruisberg; he's in the book."

DeKok quickly walked over to Vledder's desk.

"Where?" he demanded.

The young inspector pointed at a space on the fourth page.

"Here. Ronald Kruisberg, signed and written in block letters."

DeKok peered over Vledder's shoulder. The name was scribbled untidily, but legibly. He shook his head with amazement.

"But that can't be," he exclaimed. "It's unbelievable."

Vledder had a look of consternation.

"Why unbelievable?" he asked. "After all, you maintain you saw him. Well, it appears you were right. He signed the register, just like all the other mourners."

DeKok sank down in the chair behind his own desk.

"But don't you understand?" he asked tiredly. "Ronald Kruisberg is officially dead and buried. He couldn't possibly use his own name."

Vledder tapped the book in front of him.

"You wouldn't expect his name here."

DeKok scratched the back of his head.

"Not the name *Kruisberg*," he said shakily. "My hope was to find any unusual name to offer a clue for our colleagues in Antwerp. After I saw him, I also hoped, of course, I might discover the alias he is now using. But that was simply an afterthought."

Vledder shook his head.

"Perhaps there's nothing out of the ordinary. Could be Kruisberg has lived a normal life for the last twelve years, using his own name. Perhaps you overlooked something at the time."

"How and what?"

Vledder shrugged.

"How should I know? Perhaps the obituary was about somebody else with the same name. Could you have asked for the wrong Kruisberg at the registry?"

DeKok shook his head.

"I'm not that senile," he said sharply. "But it *is* an idea. Tomorrow we go to the registry office, together. You can look over my shoulder while I recheck everything carefully. There should also be a death certificate from a physician, or perhaps an autopsy report. It could nullify the cause of death as a car accident."

The phone on DeKok's desk rang. Vledder answered it, as usual. DeKok hardly ever answered his own phone. Vledder's face froze.

"What is it?" asked DeKok.

Vledder replaced the receiver.

"Guess who's downstairs and wants to come up?"

"Who?"

"Kruisberg."

3

The young man who entered the detective room was big, wide, and strong. The heavy, fur-collared coat accentuated his forceful build.

When he approached DeKok's desk, he took off his Russian-style fur hat and raked his fingers through his blond hair.

There was a smile on his face.

"You're Inspector DeKok?"

The old detective nodded.

"With a kay-oh-kay," he said, almost automatically. With a grandiose gesture he offered his visitor a chair. Meanwhile, his sharp gaze roamed over the young man's face. He searched for a resemblance, but could not find it.

"You, eh, you're Ronald Kruisberg?"

"Ronald Kruisberg," the young man confirmed.

DeKok recognized him vaguely as one of the attendees around the gravesite.

"How old are you?"

"Twenty-four."

"Married?"

The young man smiled.

"I have a girlfriend."

"Where do you live?"

"On the old Peat Market, looking over Mint Tower."

"Together with your girlfriend?"

Kruisberg looked amused, the beginning of a smile on his face.

"Surely that's not against the law?"

DeKok grimaced.

"Those are the norms of this modern age," he said somberly. "My old mother would have condemned it."

The young man laughed.

"My mother thinks it's just fine."

"Is she still alive?"

"Certainly."

"And your father?"

Kruisberg lowered his head.

"Father is dead. Two years ago he was killed in a car accident."

DeKok cocked his head.

"You have fond memories of your father?"

The young man shrugged.

"Hardly. I almost never saw him; he was always on the road, due to his business. Usually he was abroad." There was a self-conscious grin on his mouth. "He did not spend a lot of time with me."

He sounded bitter.

DeKok pulled out his lower lip and let it plop back. It was one of his more annoying, disgusting habits.

"This morning you were at a funeral at Sorrow Field?"

"Yes."

"And you signed the condolence register?"

"Yes."

"Why?"

Kruisberg looked surprised.

"The undertaker held the book out to me and gave me a pen. He told me to also write my name in block letters."

DeKok smiled.

"I meant, why did you attend the funeral of a gentleman by the name of Hendrik-Jan Assumburg?"

"Mr. Assumburg is...was my uncle. He was married to my mother's youngest sister."

DeKok nodded and glanced at Vledder, who unobtrusively was taking everything down in his own peculiar shorthand.

"You kept in close contact with him?"

Ronald Kruisberg shook his head.

"No, I usually saw Uncle Henry only on birthdays. To me he always seemed remote, a somewhat private person. He had very little contact with the family and people in general. I was under the impression my Aunt Evelyn was not really happy with him."

DeKok rubbed his chin.

"Have you any idea why your uncle was murdered in Belgium?"

Kruisberg made a helpless gesture.

"The family doesn't have a clue."

"What did your uncle do for a living?"

"He was a businessman."

DeKok grinned.

"That covers a multitude of possibilities."

Ronald Kruisberg suddenly looked sad.

"I think," he said evenly, "he was involved in the same type of nefarious activities as my father."

DeKok feigned surprise.

"Your father was involved in nefarious activities?"

The young man nodded slowly.

"So I presume. I do remember moving a lot when I was young because there were always people pursuing us for money. I had the distinct impression my father cheated people."

DeKok spread his hand, imitating the preacher at the funeral.

"*De mortuis nil nisi bene*," he said out loud. "Or in more common Dutch, speak no ill of the dead."

Ronald Kruisberg stared in the distance.

DeKok leaned comfortably back in his chair and paused for several seconds. Then he pulled himself up and leaned forward. He looked significantly at the large clock on the wall.

"You've been sitting there for almost half an hour," his voice reflecting pure wonderment, "and I still don't know the reason for your visit."

Ronald Kruisberg looked at his interrogator. The simple amiability had been wiped off his face. There were hard lines around his mouth as he glared at DeKok.

"You immediately took the initiative," he said harshly. "You never gave me a chance to bring up the reason for my visit."

DeKok bowed his head in mock shame.

"My apologies," he said. "We policemen are not known for our tact." He looked up. "But I take it you came here because there's something you want to tell us."

Young Kruisberg nodded gravely.

"When we were all standing around the gravesite and the minister was still speaking, a man suddenly ran away. You chased him."

"Yes."

"Who was that man?"

Vledder looked puzzled.

"Why?" he exclaimed excitedly. "Why did you insist that you didn't know the man who ran away? Why did you say you only ran after him because he was a pick-pocket whom you had caught in the act? That's a strange, stupid tale. You could see from Kruisberg's face he didn't believe a word of it."

DeKok accepted the criticism with resignation.

"My story wasn't all *that* strange or stupid," he defended himself weakly. "Cemeteries are pestered by pickpockets. Believe me, I know some experts."

Vledder shook his head with disapproval.

"And I maintain it was a tactical blunder. Your re-actions were totally wrong. You wasted a unique chance."

"What chance?"

The young inspector made an emotional gesture.

"You should have simply told that boy that the man who ran away was his father."

"Who has arisen from the dead?"

Vledder nodded vehemently.

"Something like that—yes! You could have come to the point, arranged a trap; in the shortest possible time you would have solved the mystery of the miraculously arisen Ronald Kruisberg."

DeKok leaned forward and leaned on his elbows. His face was a picture of cooperation and goodwill.

"Let us," he began in a friendly tone of voice, "analyze the story of young Kruisberg. Why was he so interested in the identity of the man who ran away?"

Vledder simply stared at his partner for a moment.

"Because," he said heatedly, "because he had noticed several times that the man showed an uncommon interest in him. The man had followed him through town, had hung around his house on the Peat Market. Then he showed himself at the cemetery. You'll have to admit anyone would be curious."

DeKok nodded.

"If," he said calmly, "the man was an unknown."

Vledder looked startled.

"But that is what, who, he *is*."

"Are you sure?"

The young man grinned without mirth.

"Why else would he come here to ask if you had recognized him?"

DeKok pulled out his lower lip and let it plop back. He repeated the gesture.

"Stop that," said Vledder, irked.

DeKok stopped and rubbed his chin instead.

After a long pause he offered, "If I can still recognize the elder Kruisberg after twelve years, how likely is it that his twenty-four-year-old son *doesn't* after just two years?" DeKok grinned. "Think about Mrs. Kruisberg.

I watched her during the funeral. Don't you think she would have fainted with fright to suddenly see her dead husband at her brother-in-law's gravesite?"

Vledder's face became less belligerent.

"Maybe she didn't see him."

DeKok nodded with emphasis.

"She saw him, alright," he said with authority. "She was standing right next to her son."

Vledder swallowed.

"But that means," he admitted, sheepishly, "the entire Kruisberg family knows Ronald Senior didn't really die."

DeKok nodded slowly.

"The family is now concerned to know if I recognized the old...the dead Kruisberg." He grinned maliciously. "And I would like them to worry a little longer."

For a while Vledder stared at his notes, lost in thought. He looked up after several minutes.

"How does dying make any sense?"

DeKok scratched the back of his head.

"Is that a philosophical question?"

Vledder shook his head impatiently.

"No, it is a judicial question. If the elder Kruisberg is alive, not erroneously declared deceased, what could he gain by being dead?"

DeKok grinned.

"Awkwardly put, but I know what you mean. Just think about the many people he defrauded, to whom he owes money. Sometimes dying is the only solution. In death the worldly responsibility for a misspent life is judicially absolved. You can't prosecute or sue a corpse. There's really only one way out for old Kruisberg."

"And what is that?"

"To remain dead."

4

Together, Vledder and DeKok walked out of the station house and entered the Quarter. The night was as biting as the day had been, and the water in the canals sparkled with a coating of ice. The Red Light District had slowed down because of the cold, but did not sleep entirely. No matter what the hour of the day or night, there were always people in the streets and along the canals. Likewise there were always prostitutes behind the windows of the brothels and in single rooms that formed thousands of "office" spaces devoted to their trade.

Amsterdam is a veritable labyrinth of narrow streets, small canals, quaint old bridges, dark alleys, and un-expected squares. Exotic, beautiful ladies, well-dressed pimps, and innumerable bars and eating establishments enliven and commingle with the architectural wonders. Amidst the bustling streets come the endless streams of tourists who mix with the locals of the centuries-old quarter to create an atmosphere that is beyond duplication.

DeKok looked resignedly around and greeted a few older prostitutes jovially. He waved away a young girl, new in the business, whom he did not know. A few older members of the world's oldest profession quickly admonished her.

At the corner of Barn Alley, the two shivering inspectors escaped into the warm, intimate atmosphere of Little Lowee's Bar. In contrast to outside, it was remarkably quiet in what Lowee called "his establishment."

Lowee, called "Little Lowee" because of his diminutive size, greeted them from behind the bar. His narrow, mousy face lit up with a bright smile.

"Long time no see," he chirped. "Bin scarce, eh? Too cold…too busy, what?"

DeKok hoisted himself onto a stool in front of the bar.

"As long as crime pays," he said soberly, "the police will never have a recession."

"And? Do it pay?"

DeKok grimaced.

"As never before."

Little Lowee laughed.

"Same recipe?"

Without waiting for an answer, Lowee dove under the counter and emerged with a bottle of venerable cognac, which he placed on the bar with a sigh of intense satisfaction.

"Les 'ope dat I always can stash youse a nice bottle like this in da place."

There was genuine friendliness in his voice.

DeKok offered him a warm smile.

With a series of routine movements, the small barkeep placed three large snifters on the counter and uncorked the bottle. DeKok watched intently as Lowee poured the cognac into the glasses.

He liked to spend time in Lowee's bar. He thoroughly

enjoyed the company of the man. He liked him because of his many sterling qualities and a little because of his many transgressions. At one time or another, Lowee had probably broken nearly every commandment of God and the law. But, like most denizens of the Quarter, his crimes had always been so-called clean crimes. In all those years the police had only arrested him once for a misdemeanor. There had never been any proof of a felony.

When Lowee had completed his ritual, DeKok took the snifter in the ball of his hand and gently swirled the liquid around the glass. Then he inhaled the enticing aroma deeply. He closed his eyes and an expression of pure delight transformed his face. Then he took the first, careful sip. Slowly he swallowed, and he could feel the glow of the exquisite liquor warm his entire body.

"This," he said, nodding his head, "is a slaking moment for a thirsty soul."

Lowee preened under the praise.

"DeKok," he said, "you's a poet."

DeKok took another sip and then, still warming the glass in his hand, looked around.

"Where is everybody?" he asked. "It's never been this empty."

Lowee spread out both hands.

"I thinks 'alf the Quarter is 'ome, gettin' a drunk on."

DeKok looked a question.

"Bad news?"

Lowee nodded with emphasis.

"Rickie croaked."

DeKok narrowed his eyes.

"Rickie of Apache Alia?"

The friendly face of the barkeep became sad.

"I 'eard this afternoon from some o' 'is boys. They hadda fish 'im outta dock in Antwerp."

"Murdered?"

Lowee bowed his head.

"Poisoned."

They walked back to the station house. It was less busy out, with fewer people in the streets and a lot of the windows shrouded in darkness. Even some of the sex shops were closed.

Vledder glanced at DeKok.

"Who's Rickie of Apache Alia?"

DeKok waved around, taking in the neighborhood.

"He was a man who grew up in this neighborhood. His mother's name was Alia. In the old days she lent money to the girls in the business. Interest was a quarter on the dollar."

"Twenty-five percent?"

DeKok nodded.

"But not per year, by the month."

Vledder grimaced.

"That's pure usury."

DeKok pulled up his collar. The glow of the cognac was fading.

"When she had earned enough, she bought a bar on the seadike and called it Apache Alia."

Vledder nodded to himself.

"Rickie of Apache Alia," he repeated slowly. "It

almost sounds like nobility."

DeKok smiled briefly.

"Underworld nobility."

"What did he do for a living?"

The old inspector made a sad gesture with his hand.

"Everything and nothing. He did whatever was illegal—stole, fenced, blackmailed, gambled. He also smuggled, trading in women, girls, drugs…you name it. Rickie never turned down anything. There was a rumor that he didn't even refuse a killing when asked."

"Tough customer."

"You could say that."

"Old?"

"He'd be about fifty. But he has no arrest record. In fact he's never been contacted by the police or judicial authorities."

Vledder was surprised.

"How is that possible?"

DeKok smiled patiently.

"Rickie was a smart operator. Others did his dirty work."

"And he kept the profits."

"Exactly. He inherited the mentality of his mother, profiting from other people's misery."

Vledder shook his head, "You can't do that forever without paying a heavy price. And it seems somebody finally paid him his due."

"It seems so."

Vledder suddenly gave a short, barking laugh.

"At least they didn't fish him out of an Amsterdam canal. Then we would have had to be involved."

DeKok did not react. Suddenly he turned a corner, crossed Old Church Square, and walked into one of the many side streets. Vledder followed him.

"We're not going back to the office?"

The gray sleuth pointed upward at a lit window in one of the houses.

"She's still awake."

"Who?"

"Apache Alia."

DeKok approached a green-painted door, pushed it open, and worked his two hundred pounds up the narrow staircase. The threads creaked under the weight. Vledder followed.

The narrow landing was dark. Light seeped over the threshold of one door. DeKok knocked on the door and pushed it open at the same time.

An old woman in a threadbare kimono was seated at a table near the window. In front of her on the woolen tablecloth was a silver frame surrounding the portrait of a man.

The woman looked up as the men entered the room. When she recognized DeKok, she turned the framed face down. There was an evil fire in her small green eyes.

"What are you doing here?" she snarled.

DeKok took off his hat and lowered his chin to his chest.

"I just heard from Little Lowee what happened to Rickie," he said somberly.

With a shaking motion, Alia placed her hand on the back of the portrait.

"And?"

It sounded like a challenge.

DeKok made an indecisive gesture.

"I, eh, I saw your light was still on," he said shyly. "So I thought…eh, then I thought, 'It's her son, I should express my sympathy, deliver my condolences.'"

Hesitatingly he held out his hand.

Apache Alia raised her chin in the air.

"You're not really expecting *me* to shake your hand, are you?" Her voice was harsh, hostile. "And you don't have to pull such a sadsack face, either, as if you're sorry he's dead. Don't try to tell me my Rickie was a friend of yours."

DeKok retracted his hand and shook his head.

"No. Rickie was no friend of mine, certainly not." He shrugged. "But I never bothered him in the least."

Apache Alia grimaced.

"You never had the chance!" She sounded belligerent. With a crooked finger she tapped the side of her head. "My Rickie had brains, he knew what was what. You, with your stupid police brain, couldn't touch him. He was just too smart for dumb cops."

DeKok scratched the back of his neck. He understood the bitterness of the old woman. He took a chair and sat down across the table from her. When she removed her hand momentarily, he picked up the portrait, turned it right side up, and pulled it closer.

"Are you sad, Alia?" he asked in a sympathetic voice.

Tears suddenly filled her eyes.

"Can't you tell?" She swore loudly and with venom.

DeKok nodded.

"Of course," he said softly and evenly.

For a long time he stared at the portrait. He was

familiar with the face. He had met Rickie several times in response to anonymous phone calls. The accusations were usually vague, never proven. He looked up.

"How old was Rickie?"

"Forty-eight."

"Too young to die."

Alia swallowed.

"They poisoned him." She shook her head. "Poison! You can't get more cowardly and depraved." With the back of her hand she wiped her eyes. "Rickie wasn't all that bad, not nearly as bad as people said. People portrayed him as cruel...a beast. But he wasn't like that at all, really. A mother knows her own child."

DeKok pushed the portrait back toward her.

"A mother knows," he agreed amiably.

Apache Alia pointed at the portrait on the table.

"Do you know that my boy gave a lot of money to the Salvation Army?"

DeKok shook his head.

"I did not know that."

"Deep down, Rickie was very religious. When he was small and I was still living wild, he went to parochial school. The nuns told him about God and stuff. He learned about Maria and Our Dear Lord. He never really abandoned religion after that."

DeKok coughed discreetely. He didn't know how to react to the information. Rickie of Apache Alia as a religious person was a phenomenon he could not reconcile in his mind.

"Had Rickie felt threatened lately?" he asked, all business.

Alia folded her hands and rocked slightly in her chair.

"Not really," she whispered. "But he *did* know what was going to happen to him."

DeKok gave her a searching look.

"Rickie knew?" There was disbelief in his voice.

"Before he left last week, he stopped by. Rickie was nervous, not his usual self." She looked up. "He was sitting right there, where you are sitting. I'd never seen him so tired, dispirited. I asked him if something was the matter. Then he took my hands and said, 'Mother, don't be afraid if I die. And above all, do not grieve for me.'"

DeKok took a deep breath.

"Is that what he said, Alia?"

Her head moved, hardly noticeable.

"Those were his last words to me."

5

The next morning, Inspector DeKok felt half asleep as he rode along in the streetcar he sometimes took to work. He had not slept well the night before. The face he had seen at the gravesite dominated his thoughts. Tossing and turning, he fretted if Vledder was right. Had he been mistaken in identifying the face as belonging to the long-dead Ronald Kruisberg? After all, one doesn't often meet a man who has risen from the dead. Only after finally convincing himself he had *not* made a mistake had he sunk into a deep sleep. But the sleep had been too short—all too soon the alarm clock reminded him it was time to start another day.

At the stop near Roses Canal, a heavyset woman dropped into the seat next to him. Her weight pressed against him. As the streetcar turned, he felt as if he was being flattened against the window. Across from him was a man reading a newspaper. DeKok squinted to read one of the headlines, something about there not being enough ice on the Frisian lakes, rivers, and canals to organize the Eleven-City Skating Race. He thought briefly about the race. He had attended it only once. It was a grueling race on the ice around the Province of Friesland. The skaters covered about fifty miles in the bone-chilling cold, usually accompanied by a merciless polar wind. The ice was not smooth, especially on the lakes, where ridges and other uneven places proved hazardous. He remembered thinking while he was watching the group of skaters go by that he would never submit himself to such an ordeal. Just walking outside at such a time was a test of will and determination.

When the streetcar reached Central Station, he exited with a sense of liberation. He was now only a few blocks away from the station house. He stretched to get the last few kinks out and crossed Dam Square. In front of him he saw the swaying shape of a heavyset woman. He slowed down and took a slightly diverging course. No sense in being squashed twice in one morning.

The short walk banished the last remnants of sleep. Happily humming a Christmas carol, he almost danced up the stairs to the detective room.

Vledder was already behind his desk, his fingers flying over the keyboard of his computer. DeKok hung his hat and coat on the peg and walked over to Vledder's desk.

"You look busy," he said casually.

Vledder looked up.

"I have no choice," he said somberly. "Commissaris Buitendam was waiting for me this morning. He thought our report about the funeral was too brief. He wants a complete and detailed report."

DeKok grinned.

"With a black mourning border, no doubt."

Vledder looked stony.

"You and your condolence register."

"What do you mean?"

Vledder gesticulated at his computer.

"The commissaris," he said heatedly, "now wants us to do a complete background check on all the people who signed the register."

DeKok sat down behind his own desk.

"Why?" he asked.

Vledder made a helpless gesture.

"I think he just wants to make an impression on our Belgian colleagues. He said the Antwerp police were entitled to a full and complete report; we should give them all the facts we can discover."

DeKok grinned wryly.

"He's mad," he said after a while. "There must be forty to fifty names in that register. It will take forever to run a full background check on everyone." He spread his hands. "And to what purpose?"

Vledder pushed his keyboard aside.

"In retrospect," he said sourly, "we'd have been better off if you had never asked for that book."

DeKok acted surprised.

"That's nonsense. It's a Belgian murder. The investigation is in the hands of the Antwerp police. But if I had been assigned the investigation, I would have wanted to know who was interested in the victim's funeral."

Vledder nodded agreement.

"But you had not figured we would be ordered to do the background checks."

DeKok shook his head.

"It's unusual, ridiculous. Should our Belgian colleagues find a name that interests them, *then* we can check out the particular man, or woman. But to check out everybody

in the register, without definite suspicion, that is…"
Words failed him, and he paused. Then he began again,
on a different tack. "Did you tell the commissaris about
Kruisberg Senior?"

"Yes."

"And?"

Vledder turned his head away from his partner.

"He didn't believe it."

"Didn't believe what?"

Vledder turned back and pointed at his computer.

"He didn't accept your seeing a dead Ronald
Kruisberg at the funeral of Assumburg. He looked at me
sort of funny, then said he didn't want to hear about any
such fantasies."

DeKok swallowed.

"Didn't want to know about *fantasies*?" he asked
angrily.

Vledder nodded.

"When I told him that you were absolutely convinced…that you even ran after him, he said that it wasn't
unusual for people your age to suffer from diminished
eyesight."

DeKok pressed his lips together. He felt the berserker
rage building inside him and the blood rushed to his
head. He rose from behind his desk and stormed out of
the room.

Vledder followed as quickly as possible. He knew
DeKok's confrontation with the commissaris was going
to be the same as always: DeKok shooting his mouth
off, Buitendam's veins visibly throbbing, ending with a
resounding "Out!" and DeKok slamming the door.

Vledder gave his old colleague a chiding look.

"You never learn," he reprimanded. "The police department is a semimilitaristic organization with strict chains of command. In this hierarchical setup, you are subordinate to the commissaris; it is your duty to follow his orders and directives. And *that's* the way it is."

DeKok nodded with a stubborn face.

"Fine," he growled. "But as far as I know, Buitendam has *not* been appointed as house physician."

Vledder laughed.

"Is it possible, if only in this instance, you could allow the commissaris to doubt your observations?" he asked innocently. "Let me add, I too have moments of great difficulty accepting them."

For several seconds DeKok stared evenly at Vledder. Then he pointed a finger at the young man.

"In a little while you go to Town Hall and check out the death records." It sounded curt and authoritative. "I also want a copy of the death certificate and the results of any autopsy. Above all, I want the name, or names, of the doctors involved."

Vledder nodded.

"Should I also check our own files?"

"What for?"

"Fingerprints, photos?"

DeKok shook his head.

"We have none," he said soberly. "We never got that far. If the judge advocate had not…" He did not complete the sentence, but walked over to the peg where he kept his hat and coat. He was already on his way to the door, struggling into his heavy coat, when Vledder caught up with him.

"Where are you going?"

DeKok turned half around.

"I'm going to ask the widow Kruisberg if she has seen any ghosts."

DeKok left the city in the direction of Diemen, via Hartveld Bridge. It had taken a bit of doing to discover Mrs. Kruisberg's whereabouts. She had changed addresses often in the last few years. According to the latest information, her most recent move was to Polderland, south of Diemen.

By his own admission, DeKok was the worst driver in the Netherlands. He was usually driving in the wrong gear, and when he did change gears the old VW groaned and screeched in protest. When he reached Diemen he had to stop several times to get closer directions, but after a meandering trip through several streets and two near misses with other motorists, he reached Polderland. It turned out to be a new, intimate neighborhood of one- and two-story houses built with yellow bricks. The houses gave a friendly impression.

DeKok parked the VW, crooked and partly on the curb, and ambled along the street to number 723.

When he reached the door, he noticed that there was no nameplate next to the doorbell. He hesitated a moment and then rang the bell. The door was opened by a tall, distinguished woman in a tight black dress. The gray sleuth estimated her to be in her late forties. Sharp lines and wrinkles showed on her somewhat square face. There was a lot of gray in her dark hair. In response to the questioning look, DeKok bowed slightly.

"My name is DeKok," he said in a friendly tone of voice, "with a kay-oh-kay. I'm an inspector attached to Warmoes Street station in Amsterdam. About twelve years ago I was investigating a fraud case involving your husband."

She reacted in a contentious manner.

"My husband is dead," she said curtly, and attempted to close the front door.

DeKok extended an arm and prevented her from closing the door. He nodded calmly.

"I have heard your husband is deceased. I just wanted to talk with you for a moment."

Mrs. Kruisberg shook her head.

"I have no need to speak with anyone," she said icily, "and that includes you."

DeKok gave her a sharp look.

"About your son."

The expression on her face changed.

"What's the matter with my son?"

"He came to visit me."

"Why?"

"He wanted to talk to me about a strange man who's constantly following him, keeping him under surveillance."

Mrs. Kruisberg gave him a long, searching look. After a slight hesitation she opened the door farther, indicating to DeKok he could enter.

The living room was cozily furnished. Around a round table were four light blue easy chairs with white lace antimacassars on the backs. A sideboard was tastefully decorated with fine vases and glasswork. Sunny landscapes in light colors decorated the walls.

DeKok looked around, pleasantly surprised. The warm, friendly interior was in marked contrast to the cool attitude of his hostess. He sank down in one of the easy chairs and placed his hat on the carpet next to him.

"You've moved a good deal," he began with surprise in his voice.

Mrs. Kruisberg sat down across from him. There was a bitter smile around her mouth.

"It was flight...a constant flight from the ghosts of the past."

"How do you mean?"

"You must know my husband had a past. I did not know what kind of business he did when I married him. I thought I had chosen a respectable businessman for a husband...he turned out to be a swindler."

DeKok looked her in the eyes.

"That sounds bitter."

Mrs. Kruisberg nodded her agreement.

"It was a bitter disappointment. Perhaps it would have been better if I had divorced him as soon as I found out about his crooked practices. But I lacked the courage."

"So you stayed with him."

She lowered her head somewhat.

"We had just celebrated our twenty-fifth wedding anniversary. Then, perhaps in part because of you, the ground became too hot under his feet. He fled abroad."

She sighed deeply. "Me he left with a mountain of debt and a difficult son."

"That would be Ronald?"

"Yes."

"And you never heard from your husband?"

"We saw neither hide nor hair. At first I was afraid to move, thinking if things calm down, he'll be back and need to know where to find us. But the years went by and the pressure of the creditors increased until it became unbearable. People thought I was an accomplice in the swindles and that I was still in contact with him. They wanted me to pay." She made a helpless gesture. "Pay with what? I had nothing! I was too frightened to approach the welfare administration. But we had to live. To provide for my son and myself, I took a job as the secretary for a ship chandler. Once I became employed, I moved several times to shake the many creditors."

DeKok nodded.

"When did you hear from your husband again?"

"About five years ago."

DeKok spread out both hands.

"That must have been hard. I mean, with that many changes of address, it must have been difficult for him to find you."

She shook her head.

"He did not find me."

DeKok looked startled.

"He did not find you?" he asked.

Again the bitter smile.

"I heard he was still alive."

"How?"

She did not answer at once. She moved uneasily in her chair.

"My youngest sister, Evelyn, met a man during a ski vacation in St. Moritz, Switzerland. He was apparently financially secure, a businessman. Although the man was almost twenty years older than my sister, she was attracted to him and they married within six months after they met."

DeKok looked up at her.

"Hendrik-Jan Assumburg?"

She nodded.

"Henry."

"The man who was buried yesterday?"

"Indeed."

DeKok rubbed his chin.

"And that was the man who said that Ronald was still alive?"

Mrs. Kruisberg nodded again.

"They were married in Switzerland. After the honey-moon, Evelyn came to see me, to introduce Henry. At the time Henry said he knew a Ronald Kruisberg. He, Henry, had met the man in Antwerp, a member of some kind of religious sect, or cult." She paused. "The news didn't affect me much. The name Kruisberg is not unusual. Besides, the idea of my husband as a member of some kind of cult seemed unbelievable. To make sure, though, I showed him a photograph of Ronald."

"And?"

"According to Henry there was no doubt the man he met in Antwerp was the same man who had left me seven years before."

"Then you traveled to Antwerp?"

She slowly shook her head.

"I did not want to go," she said resignedly. "After all those years I had not the least desire to pick up where we had left off. The mere thought of living with that man again was...was...abhorrent to me. So I took no steps to contact him." She gripped her head with both hands and sighed deeply. "Two years ago, I heard from Belgium that he had died in a car accident. It was liberating. I felt a load had been lifted off my shoulders."

"Where was Ronald buried?"

"It was his wish to be buried at Sorrow Field in Amsterdam."

"Near where Hendrik-Jan Assumburg is buried?"

She made a languid gesture.

"The graves," she said softly, "are barely a hundred feet apart."

DeKok leaned his head in the palm of his hand and thought.

"Who was the charming gentleman who gave your sister so much, eh, support during the funeral?"

"A friend."

"Whose friend?"

"Evelyn and Henry's."

"A close friend?"

"More or less."

DeKok did not ask anything for a long period. Both he and his hostess remained silent.

A pendulum clock on the chimney mantel ticked away the minutes. Outside, in the garden, a pair of chickadees fluttered around a seed ball hanging from a thread.

Suddenly DeKok leaned forward.

"Mrs. Kruisberg," he whispered, "do you ever see ghosts?"

With a shock she looked up.

"Ghosts?" she repeated.

DeKok nodded seriously.

"Ghosts, specters, spirits, apparitions—as if someone who's been dead for years has suddenly arisen from the dead."

Mrs. Kruisberg acted confused. Her lower lip began to quiver.

"Who…who has arisen?"

DeKok cocked his head and carefully noted every movement of her skin, eyes, and mouth.

"Ronald Kruisberg…your husband."

She looked at him with large frightened eyes. Suddenly her entire body shook, intensely, out of control.

Waving both arms over her head she began to scream.

"I don't want it! I don't want him to live…I don't want him to live…I don't want…"

She repeated it like an echo.

6

Vledder looked at DeKok with surprise.

"That's what she said?

The gray sleuth nodded.

"'I don't want him to live.' She kept repeating it. When she finally fell silent she was so confused, completely exhausted, I couldn't get any sense out of her. She was hysterical, no longer accessible to me."

"Then you left?"

DeKok shrugged.

"I could not calm her down. And I didn't want to leave her alone in that condition. I thought that was a bit dangerous. I finally got the name of her house doctor. I called him and as soon as he was there, I sneaked out of the house."

"Like a thief in the night."

"Something like that—I wasn't proud of it."

"And what do you make of her behavior?"

DeKok shrugged again.

"It was so intense, so very insistent. A scream of intense desire, you understand? She wanted him dead. But all the time, I feel, she knew in her heart of hearts Ronald Kruisberg never really died."

"How?"

"What do you mean?"

"How does she know he's still alive?"

DeKok spread wide both of his hands.

"I think, like me, she saw him at the cemetery. She may have had earlier indications he was alive." He sighed. "I wanted to ask her all that, but, as I said, I never had the chance."

Vledder shook his head, deep in thought.

"Isn't it strange," he said slowly, "Henry Assumburg knew Ronald Kruisberg when he was alive." He looked up at DeKok. "Do you think it's why Kruisberg came to Sorrow Field?"

"To attend the funeral, you mean?"

"Yes."

DeKok scratched the back of his neck.

"That would indicate," he said hesitatingly, "some sort of emotional bond between the two men...some sort of relationship. You have to keep in mind Kruisberg ran a great risk by appearing in person."

Vledder nodded agreement.

"You're saying that Assumburg and Kruisberg Senior knew each other well. That is to say, there were closer connections than just a chance meeting."

DeKok slapped the top of his desk with a flat hand.

"It's all just too far-fetched," he said crossly. "Evelyn, Mrs. Kruisberg's younger sister, just happens to be in Switzerland. There she meets a man, who just happens to know the long-disappeared, meanwhile-deceased Kruisberg. The same Kruisberg just happens to arise from the dead to attend the funeral of Assumburg. Of course nobody recognizes him...except me."

Vledder laughed.

"Now do you understand why the commissaris calls it nonsense?"

DeKok growled.

"That's just an easy escape."

"An escape?" repeated Vledder.

DeKok nodded, still angry.

"An escape for the dim-witted—labeling something 'nonsense' is easy. There's no longer any need to try to understand." He looked up. "Have you checked out the central register?"

"Yes."

"And? Come on, tell me."

Vledder opened his notebook.

"You were right, Ronald Kruisberg is officially listed as deceased."

"Cause of death?"

"Vehicular. It seems he ran a fast car into a concrete wall in Antwerp."

DeKok was surprised.

"In Antwerp?"

"According to the record."

DeKok grinned sardonically.

"Rickie of Apache Alia died in Antwerp. Hendrik-Jan Assumburg died in Antwerp. Now, it seems, Ronald Kruisberg also died in Antwerp." DeKok shook his head. "Dying in Antwerp…it looks like an epidemic."

Vledder looked up from his notebook.

"That's true," he agreed. "But with one distinct difference: Assumburg and Rickie were both fished out of the water, already dead. Kruisberg died accidentally.

He was burned to death."

DeKok narrowed his eyes.

"Was he?"

Vledder became a bit agitated.

"That's what it states in the record." He took a deep breath and visibly calmed down. "But I understand, DeKok," he said with a twinge of regret, "everything stands or falls with your observation at the cemetery."

"And you still doubt that?"

Vledder did not answer. He was deep in thought. After a long pause he nodded to himself.

"We have to go to Antwerp," he said.

Adjutant Kamphuis, in his usual hurry, bustled into the detective room and approached DeKok. He dropped a fax on his desk with an insistent gesture.

"Actually, Buitendam should have given you this order," he apologized. "But the commissaris is on leave for a few days."

DeKok looked up.

"Is that possible?"

"What?"

"The commissaris on leave. I thought nobody could get on without him around here, even for a day."

Kamphuis grinned.

"That's why the order comes through me."

"What kind of order?"

The adjutant pointed at the fax.

"To attend a funeral."

DeKok grimaced.

"Can't you find someone else to do it? Vledder and I are still struggling with the aftermath of a similar assignment."

"Attending a funeral?"

"Exactly."

Kamphuis nodded calmly.

"Well, you see...you two have experience."

He turned around and walked away.

DeKok reluctantly picked up the fax.

"You are requested," he read out loud, "to attend the burial of Richard Strijdbaar at 11:00, this coming Wednesday. Services will be held at Sorrow Field Cemetery in Amsterdam. Richard Strijdbaar is the victim of a murder, and his body was found in the waters beneath Bonaparte Dock near Aldegonde Quay in Antwerp. Please forward any pertinent details to H. J. M. Opdenbroecke, Chief Commissaris of the Judicial Police, Antwerp." He placed the notice in a drawer of his desk. "It is signed by J. A. E. M. Mannekes, King's Prosecutor."

Vledder frowned.

"Who is Richard Strijdbaar?"

DeKok smiled.

"It's the real name of Rickie from Apache Alia."

Vledder maneuvered the VW through Old Bridge Alley toward Damrak with difficulty. He shifted smoothly, without any undue noise, but he could tell DeKok had recently driven the much-abused vehicle. Near Mint Square they got stuck in a traffic backup.

Vledder put the vehicle in neutral, keeping his foot on the gas pedal while fiddling with the inadequate heating controls. He hoped against hope the increased RPMs would increase the heat delivered by the air-cooled engine.

DeKok rubbed his cold hands together.

"You think there will be an Eleven-City Race this year?"

Vledder honked the horn several times. He was always irritated in traffic jams.

"Who knows," he snarled, "maybe it'll freeze and maybe it'll thaw." He looked aside. "Why do you want to visit the minister?"

DeKok made a negligent gesture.

"I have questions about his sermon."

"The one in the chapel, or the one at the gravesite?"

"It's about the sermon in the chapel. *De mortuis nil nisi bene,*" said DeKok with an atrocious accent. "About the dead, nothing but good, or rather, speak no ill of the dead. You see, it wasn't so much what he said that caught my attention but the meaning I seemed to hear in his words. I just couldn't get rid of the idea he wanted to make something specifically clear."

Vledder shook his head in disapproval.

"Surely you don't want to get involved in that Belgian murder?"

DeKok looked surprised.

"I certainly do. You do too, remember? You said yourself we had to go to Antwerp. Besides, like it or not, I think we're already into this case pretty deep."

Vledder took a deep breath.

"Yes, I did say we needed to go to Antwerp for Ronald Kruisberg...because I want to know for sure whether or not the guy is alive. I couldn't care less about Assumburg," he said vehemently. "Or Rickie," he continued. "I'm furious we have to go to his funeral as well. Why don't we just let the Belgians take care of their own business? They're certainly capable. Hercule Poirot was a Belgian, after all."

DeKok laughed out loud.

"Yes, he was," he admitted. "He was better than you and I together."

Whatever had been blocking traffic must have moved, because the backup slowly started to move. With a sigh of relief, Vledder engaged first gear. They made good progress as they proceeded to Amsterdam-South. On Crib Street they stopped and exited the car. They crossed a wide sidewalk and approached a brown lacquered door with glass-in-lead insets. There was a discreet white enamel sign with black letters to the left of the door.

"Vicarage," read DeKok, "of the Freethinking Dutch Reformed Protestant Church." He pressed the bell.

"My, my," said DeKok while they waited, and he read the sign again, "these folks are against everyone, aren't they? 'Freethinking' must mean they're prepared to reject any idea. 'Dutch' must exclude all foreign churches. Then 'reformed' seems to say they're different from the Protestants, who are protesters by definition; the Protestants protested against the Catholic Church."

"Don't be so naive," countered Vledder. "This is one of the largest denominations in the Netherlands, something like the Unitarian Church in the United States.

They worship God, but are against the traditional rituals and the strict hierarchy in other churches. It could be *your* church, very understanding of your rebellious nature."

"I know, but I've always wanted to make that remark about this church. It's the devil in me, I suppose."

In the door opening, dressed in faded jeans and a gray sweater, the reverend looked a lot less distinguished than in the formal black suit he'd worn at the funeral.

He looked from DeKok to Vledder and back again.

"How can I help you, gentlemen?"

His voice sounded unsure.

The gray sleuth smiled.

"My name is DeKok," he said amiably, "with a kay-oh-kay." He pointed at Vledder. "This is my colleague, Vledder. We're inspectors."

"Police?"

DeKok nodded with conviction.

"We would like to talk to you about the many facets of your profession."

The man visibly dropped his uncertainty. He straightened up and stuck out his chin.

"The ministry is not a profession," he said severely. "It is a calling. One is *called* to the ministry." He paused and evaluated the two men. "You're here for spiritual guidance?"

It sounded like a joke.

DeKok shook his head.

"I'm afraid," he said sadly, "your spiritual guidance would be wasted on us. You see, we're children of Satan."

The minister smiled indulgently.

"It's that bad?"

DeKok made a melancholy gesture.

"The moment a person becomes part of the police, he pawns his soul to the Devil."

The minister showed surprise.

"But I always thought that the police were there to make sure people honor God's commandments?"

DeKok nodded.

"And that creates the difficulty, the dichotomy," he said somberly. "If Satan didn't entice people to follow a path of mischief, we would be out of a job." He made an apologetic gesture. "It is an unhappy observation, but we owe our existence to the Devil."

Vledder grinned.

"He who pays the piper calls the tune."

The eyes of the minister lit up with pleasure. He showed a real appreciation for the banter of the two men.

"Our points of view are thus predetermined," he laughed. "I speak for God and you two speak for the Devil." He stepped aside and beckoned. "Although one doesn't lightly invite the Devil into one's house, come in."

The minister led the way to a comfortable office with a rolltop desk, walls covered with books, and a set of leather Empire armchairs. He waved an invitation.

Once Vledder and DeKok were seated, he took a seat opposite them.

"I have not yet introduced myself," he said in a friendly tone of voice. "My name is Wiebe Sijbertsma, but I assume you already knew that. I also assume, in contrast to our amusing exchange at the front door, your visit has a more serious purpose." He narrowed his eyes slightly. "If I remember correctly, I have seen you gentlemen at Sorrow Field Cemetery. Did you not attend the funeral of, ah, Mr. Assumburg?"

DeKok nodded agreement.

"That is correct. The Antwerp police asked us to attend the funeral. Assumburg was murdered in Antwerp, you see. It was a routine matter—we did not expect any surprises."

"But there were surprises?"

DeKok pulled out his lower lip and let it plop back. When he saw the minister grimace, he desisted.

"Yes," he said. "Near the gravesite I saw a man who has been dead for two years."

"Remarkable."

"To be sure."

Sijbertsma pursed his lips.

"You *did* create a little commotion when you suddenly pursued him."

DeKok lowered his head.

"Please accept my apologies. I had no intention of disturbing the ceremony." He looked up. His sharp eyes kept the face of the minister trapped. "However I was struck by your sermon at the chapel, more than I was by the sudden confrontation with the living dead."

"Why so?"

"Much to my surprise you clearly indicated the life of the deceased...how shall I say it? You said Assumburg's lifestyle raised some questions."

"You are correct."

DeKok smiled.

"I presume that you weighed your words carefully. I don't want to accept the view that your remarks about Assumburg's life and deeds were prompted by ill will."

Minister Sijbertsma steepled his hands in front of his chest.

"You are again correct," he said pensively. "My sermon, my eulogy if you will, deviated from the usual. The fact is, someone requested it be that way."

For a moment DeKok seemed stunned.

"It was by request?"

"Yes."

"By whom?"

"Mr. Assumburg."

"What?"

Minister Sijbertsma spread his hands and nodded.

"Exactly fourteen days before his death, he visited me, here at the vicarage. He was sitting there, in the same chair you're sitting in. He asked me if I was prepared to adorn his eulogy."

DeKok's mouth fell open.

"Meaning embellish?"

The minister nodded, outwardly unmoved.

"He used the word *adorn*."

7

For several seconds, DeKok merely stared at the Reverend Sijbertsma. The old inspector's face was expressionless.

"How did you respond? At the very least it was an unusual request."

The minister leaned back in his chair and nodded.

"It was. My first reaction was confusion, and I asked him if he wanted to use me for some kind of practical joke. But Mr. Assumburg assured me sincerely that although his choice of words might be construed as frivolous, his request was made in good faith."

DeKok, for the first time, looked at Vledder. The young man was studiously and unobtrusively writing in his notebook. DeKok was pleased. No doubt the information would find its way into Vledder's computer, but long ago DeKok had impressed on his protégée the importance of careful notes, at all times.

He returned his attention to their host.

"What was his motivation?"

"In my opinion his motive was abundantly clear. Otherwise I would not have agreed to his suggestion."

DeKok still showed no expression.

"How much did he pay you?"

Sijbertsma became angry.

"That is an improper remark," he said furiously. "I'm not for sale."

DeKok was unmoved by the outburst.

"How much money did he give you?"

Sijbertsma lowered his gaze.

"Financially, our congregation is in bad shape," he said somberly. "Everywhere, including here, the church seems to take a less important place in people's lives. And that means a reduction of income." He sighed. "Mr. Assumburg did, indeed, pay me a sum of money." His tone changed, became more emotional. "But that was *not* the reason I agreed to his request."

"What was the reason?"

"As I said, it was his motivation. He confessed contritely to living a less than blameless life. On the contrary, his life's history contained many black pages. He had, he said, cheated his fellow man and had used many dishonest, underhanded tactics to separate them from their wealth."

"Just an ordinary grifter."

"I'm not familiar with your terminology."

DeKok ignored the remark.

"How did he swindle people? What kind of methods did he use?"

Sijbertsma shrugged his shoulders.

"I did not discuss details with him."

"Why not?"

"They didn't interest me."

DeKok grinned.

"His many victims were of no concern to you?"

Again the minister bowed his head.

"I have to confess that I did not think about possible

victims at that moment. I was primarily interested in a person who wanted to confess his sins."

"And Assumburg wanted to do that?"

He nodded emphatically.

"Absolutely. I sensed in him a clear need to sacrifice. For a worldly judge, he said, it was too late. I have not that much time left. The only thing left for me, he said, is to petition God."

"To ask God's forgiveness?"

"Exactly."

"With you as go-between?"

"Yes."

"Why did he come to you? Why didn't he visit a priest? The Roman Catholic Church is in the business of hearing confessions and giving absolution—you are not."

"We recognize testimony before God. As to why he came to me, I do not know; perhaps he had not grown up as a Roman Catholic. I just don't know why he came to me."

DeKok rubbed the bridge of his nose with his little finger.

"How did Assumburg know that he had little time left?"

"I asked him that."

"And?"

"He wasn't very clear. He said he'd had certain indications his life was going to be cut short."

DeKok shook his head in bewilderment.

"Did he know his murderer?"

Sijbertsma shook his head.

"He knew the hour of his death."

"Did he tell you that?"

The Reverend Sijbertsma did not answer at once. He suddenly turned as pale as a ghost and his hands shook.

"No," he said finally, "Assumburg told me the exact date of his burial."

From the vicarage they drove back to Warmoes Street. The minister's words echoed in their heads, slowing their thought processes. It was too fantastic, too absurd, too strange for an intellectual approach. Vledder was the first to break the silence.

"What sort of man," he said fervently, "orders a minister to *alter* his own eulogy?"

DeKok grinned.

"That's easy," he said. "You heard it yourself, an Assumburg kind of man."

Vledder slapped the steering wheel of the VW.

"Perhaps the minister was right, after all. Perhaps it was the man's idea of a practical joke."

DeKok grunted.

"You can hardly call murder a joke, not even a practical joke."

Vledder gesticulated with one hand.

"Look, if I knew I was going to be murdered, right down to the exact time, I'd take steps, wouldn't you? I'd alert the police...leave for another country—*something!*"

DeKok shrugged.

"Perhaps Assumburg was reconciled to his fate. He might have felt his death was inevitable."

Vledder shook his head.

"I don't believe that," he said stubbornly. "Every person clings to life...holds on to life with his, or her, last breath. Why should Assumburg be an exception?"

DeKok lowered himself in the seat.

"What do we really know about the man?" he asked calmly. "We do not know any of the circumstances of his life. Perhaps some of his many victims had condemned him to death and he knew the verdict."

Despite his irritation, Vledder smiled.

"And he went as a sheep to the slaughter?"

DeKok ignored the mocking undertone.

"Perhaps he was just tired of living," he philosophized. "Who knows, he could have had an incurable disease, in which case he would have looked upon death as a solution."

Vledder suddenly sat a bit straighter behind the wheel.

"That's it," he exclaimed enthusiastically.

"What?"

"Death as a solution—no, death as liberation. *That* is the right answer, DeKok. It explains everything. It wasn't murder, but suicide. Don't you see? Assumburg could control everything by killing himself. He could, indeed, determine the time of his death and arrange his funeral."

DeKok looked at his younger colleague.

"Very nice, very ingenious," he said with admiration. "Suicide does answer many questions. It even explains the need to confess, as the Reverend Sijbertsma told us." He paused and his voice became more somber. "It's just too bad that the Antwerp police insist it was murder, hence the request to attend the funeral."

"Perhaps the circumstances surrounding the discovery were not very clear. So they figured, better call it a murder rather than regret it later. It was a means to cover all the bases."

DeKok did not respond. They were almost back to the station house before he spoke again.

"I agree with you."

Vledder looked puzzled.

"Agree with what?"

"We have to go to Antwerp."

As the inspectors entered the lobby of the police station, Meindert Post, the watch commander, called them over in his habitual stentorian voice.

"Well, Meindert," said DeKok, "I'm surprised you ever use a radio. Surely you can reach anybody in the Quarter by just whispering their name."

The watch commander ignored the jibe.

"Somebody's waiting for you upstairs."

"Who?"

"A gentleman...member of the fashionable set."

DeKok gripped his chest and looked shocked.

"A *gentleman* in Warmoes Street?"

There was a dramatic disbelief in his voice.

"Just cut the theatricals, DeKok. A gentleman is what I said, and a gentleman is what he is."

"Did you ask his name?"

"Of course," Post glanced at his logbook. "His name is Ravenswood—Robert Antoine van Ravenswood."

"A name like that announces him as a gentleman, indeed."

DeKok turned away from the counter and climbed the stairs with Vledder.

A man was seated on the bench in the corridor outside the detective room. DeKok looked down at him, studying him carefully. Meindert Post was right, he concluded. The man looked like a gentleman. He looked to be a well-preserved man in his fifties, dressed in an immaculate gray suit, a red carnation in his lapel. The gray sleuth recognized the man from the gravesite. He was the man who had been such an attentive escort to the young woman in the black veil.

His legs spread, DeKok stood in front of the bench.

"Mr. Ravenswood?"

The man stood up.

"Yes, *van* Ravenswood is my name." For a moment it looked as if he had been startled, but he controlled himself immediately. "And you are the famous Inspector DeKok."

DeKok grinned.

"Infamous, more likely."

Mr. van Ravenswood's dark brown eyes gleamed. There was the hint of a smile below his thin moustache.

"Your ingenuity is virtually legendary."

DeKok ignored the praise. He determined he'd watch himself with Mr. van Ravenswood. He turned around and led the way into the detective room. While he hung up his coat and hat he invited his visitor to sit on the chair next to his desk. Then he walked around the desk and sat down himself.

"How can I be of service?"

Mr. van Ravenswood turned toward him. His browned face became serious.

"I come here on behalf of Evelyn. I mean the widow Assumburg. I take care of her business."

"You're a lawyer?"

Van Ravenswood shook his head.

"No, not at all—I'm on the board of directors of a number of concerns. But Evelyn, I mean the widow Assumburg, has asked me to assist her. It is for a young woman under these sad circumstances obviously very difficult to..." He cleared his throat and continued. "Mr. Assumburg was a wealthy man. He owned a substantial residence at Emperor's Canal and a large villa in the country, where the couple spent little time. He also had a seaworthy yacht and a substantial balance at Ijsselstein Bank."

DeKok listened intently.

"And?" he prompted.

Mr. van Ravenswood looked depressed.

"There's nothing left."

"Nothing?"

"No. The yacht is gone, and both houses are heavily mortgaged. The payments are so high Evelyn is unable to meet them. Just the interest is out of her reach. Also, the balance at the bank has disappeared."

DeKok made a dismissive gesture.

"Perhaps Mr. Assumburg did some serious gambling, even recently."

Van Ravenswood shook his head forcefully.

"I've known Henry Assumburg for years. Since before

he married Evelyn. He was not an extravagant man. On the contrary, Henry was always extremely careful, especially in financial matters. He never took any risks."

"The Assumburgs were married and held their property in common? I mean, there was no pre- or post-nuptial agreement?"

"No, nothing of the kind. They owned everything jointly."

"And before they married, there were no mortgages on the properties?"

Van Ravenswood nodded.

"I see what you mean. Evelyn would have had to be informed about any mortgages. She does recall that about fourteen days before his death, Henry had her sign a number of official-looking papers." He made a despairing gesture. "You know how trusting some wives can be. Evelyn wasn't knowledgeable about business, so she was disinterested. One might say she was careless. She cannot remember what kind of papers they were." He sighed deeply. "Legally, I'm sure it's all correct. Mortgage bankers are very careful. They don't do things on the spur of the moment. I can't help wondering what happened to the money. Just the villa in the country currently carries a mortgage of more than a million euros."

DeKok rubbed the bridge of his nose with his little finger.

"At the funeral," he said slowly, "in the chapel, the preacher made a few remarks that seemed to indicate Mr. Assumburg had led an, eh, an eventful life. Would it be possible that he was aware of his imminent death and decided to donate his assets to charity?"

Van Ravenswood grinned. It was a strange, crooked grin that gave his handsome face an impish expression.

"Henry and charity?" he exclaimed. "My dear Inspector DeKok, a greater contrast is unimaginable. The two just don't go together."

DeKok smiled faintly.

"You say you have known Mr. Assumburg for years. Have you any idea why he would need to liquidate his assets for cash?"

"Perhaps he was being blackmailed."

"By whom?"

"His murderer."

DeKok nodded slowly to himself.

"Has Mrs. Assumburg been interviewed by the Antwerp police regarding his death?"

Van Ravenswood shook his head.

"Not yet. She did receive a friendly invitation. Tomorrow we travel to Antwerp." He reached for an inside pocket and handed DeKok a letter. "Mrs. Assumburg has authorized me to report a case of forgery and fraud."

DeKok cocked his head at his visitor.

"*Forgery* and fraud?"

"Yes, both. Someone closed his bank account and took the cash—the day *after* his death."

8

Once the distinguished gentleman Robert Antoine van Ravenswood left, Vledder pointed at the complaint form in front of him. Upon DeKok's instruction, he had taken custody of the letter. Next he'd completed the official charge sheet, charging "parties unknown" with forgery and fraud.

"What do we do with this?"

"Investigate."

"Why? We're homicide. Why don't we just send it to the financial police or, better yet, forward it to the Antwerp police? They are the ones who are handling Assumburg's murder."

DeKok shook his head.

"The money was taken here in the Netherlands, from a Dutch bank. This is entirely a Dutch affair."

"But it is not *our* affair."

"No?"

Vledder reacted with his usual agitation.

"If it *is* a Dutch affair, it's still not a homicide case. And if it has something to do with a homicide, it's a case for the Belgian police. But for a Belgian murder, there would have been no question of forgery. The murderer must have taken the money and other papers from his victim. On the papers he undoubtedly found Assumburg's signature. He had only to practice signing his signature. The rest was child's play."

"Think so?"

Vledder nodded emphatically.

"That's self-evident. All of Assumburg's money has been withdrawn from the bank."

DeKok bit his lower lip and shook his head.

"It isn't all that simple," he said pensively. "The murderer ran a great risk presenting himself as Assumburg. With the sum involved, he might have been asked for additional identification. Also, some employee of the bank might have known Assumburg personally. If the fraud were detected, he would have immediately been charged with the murder as well."

"How do you mean?"

"He certainly would have to explain how he came into possession of the papers of the murdered Assumburg. I know money has a tendency to blind people, but for a murderer who had planned his deed some time before—"

Vledder interrupted.

"How do you know the murder was planned?"

DeKok looked surprised at the question.

"Assumburg *knew* he was going to be killed. Maybe someone leaked the plan…or the murderer threatened him."

"So you're abandoning my suicide theory?"

DeKok shrugged.

"The withdrawal of Assumburg's bank balance *after* his death sort of puts the suicide on shaky ground." He paused and scratched the back of his neck. "Like van Ravenswood, I do wonder what happened to all the money from the mortgages."

"That went to his blackmailer."

"It also went to his murderer?"

"Sure, why not."

DeKok looked doubtful.

"Usually a blackmailer doesn't kill the goose that lays the golden egg. Add to that the fact I don't believe the blackmail theory. Assumburg made a living out of crime rather openly. A man like that is not an easy mark."

Vledder threw his hands into the air.

"Then what?" he asked gloomily.

DeKok did not answer him. He leaned forward and rested his chin in the palms of his hands. He stared into the distance.

After a long silence he began to speak slowly.

"It just doesn't make any sense," he mused. "There's no obvious connection, and there are too many gaps. What we have so far defies any kind of logic: Henry Assumburg orders a minister to adorn the truth at his funeral. He has his wife sign some documents, heavily mortgaging his properties. He cheerfully travels to meet his murderer. As if in passing, the killer withdraws all the cash from the Assumburg bank account." He shook his head slowly. "Dick Vledder," he concluded, "this stinks to high heaven."

Slowly he rose from his chair.

"Tomorrow we're going to visit Ijsselstein Bank. We still have a few contacts there from the past. Perhaps they can tell us how the murderer acted while he cashed out the accounts."

Vledder nodded meekly.

"That's tomorrow, what are we going to do now?"

DeKok glanced at the large clock on the wall. It was past eleven. Suddenly he grinned.

"How about a cognac?"

Little Lowee looked pleasantly surprised when the two inspectors entered his intimate bar. Then he quickly wiped his hands on his soiled vest. With raised eyebrows he came from behind the counter and approached DeKok.

"You ain't sick, is youse?" he asked, worried.

DeKok smiled.

"Why, Lowee?"

Lowee pointed around the bar.

"Two times youse show inna week. It ain't 'appened in years, months anyways. So, wassa matta, youse ran outta work? Them wise guys onna strike or what?"

DeKok grinned.

"If that were only true. Then we could spend a few days here. Personally, I hope they'll organize into a union."

"Aw, come on, DeKok, a for-real union widda prezident anna secetry and all?"

"Sure. The change is badly needed. The underworld is the only group without a forty-hour work week."

Lowee grinned.

"I tink I'll purpose dat." He held out his hand. "How's about a small durnation for da strike fund?"

DeKok laughingly ignored the hand. He hoisted himself onto a bar stool next to Vledder while Lowee slipped behind the bar to complete the ceremony with the bottle and the snifters.

"Proost," said Lowee, "onna long life full o' crime."

DeKok raised his glass.

"But only with a well-organized trade union."

The barkeep took a careful sip of the splendid liquor and then replaced the glass on the bar. Confidentially he leaned closer to DeKok. His friendly, mousy face became somber.

"Youse gonna go to da funeral?"

"Whose funeral?"

"Rickie. They brung 'im to Mokum. Tomorra he's gonna be planted at Sorrow Field. I gotta invite."

Mokum is the underworld word for Amsterdam. Nobody seems to know the roots of the word. Lowee generally spoke Bargoens, the language of thieves—a mixture of Dutch, Cockney, Yiddish, and Papiamento. Papiamento was the language of the Dutch Antilles, a mixture of Dutch, Portuguese, and several African dialects. Bargoens is almost impossible to understand. DeKok was fluent in it; but lately Lowee had cleaned up his language as much as possible, for Vledder's benefit. He still spoke an atrocious Dutch, but at least it was generally understandable. It had not always been that way. There was a time when Lowee delighted in speaking straight Bargoens with DeKok all the time while studiously ignoring Vledder. It made for some interesting conversations. Lowee would be rattling away, and DeKok would respond in proper Dutch. It was like listening to one side of a telephone conversation.

"Me, too," said DeKok.

"Youse, too? Apache Alia done invited *you*?"

The inspector shook his head.

"No, I've been invited by the Belgian police."

Lowee shook his head in puzzlement.

"They's figurin' onna heibel?"

DeKok shrugged his shoulders.

"No, I don't think they expect trouble," he explained. "It's more or less customary for police to attend the funeral of a murder victim. Keep an eye on who's interested. Some killers have the uncontrollable urge to attend the funerals of their victims."

"Stupid," was Lowee's comment.

DeKok slowly rocked the glass in his hand, warming the cognac.

"You heard anything?"

"About Rickie bein' wacked?"

"Yes."

The barkeep looked around the bar, then he leaned closer.

"Rickie was broke."

DeKok grimaced.

"Rickie?" he said, disbelief in his voice. "That's hard to believe."

Lowee nodded with emphasis. His face was serious.

"I heard. Apache Alia done tol' me. You knows, Rickie ain't never bin married. He ain't got nobody. Alia izzada onliest 'eir. She done some askin' around."

"And?"

Lowee pulled his thumb from underneath his chin.

"Nuttin'. She run to city hall. Them five houses Rickie got a coupla days before 'e gone peiger, they ain't 'is no more."

"They were sold a few days before he died?"

"Yup."

"What about a last will and testament?"

"Nope, nuttin' onna paper."

"Cash?"

"Notta nickel."

DeKok grinned without mirth.

"But how is that possible? Rickie made tons of money, especially the last few years."

Lowee spread both hands wide.

"Well, there ain't nuttin' to find. Alia says there was nuttin' but letters askin' for dough anna lotsa unpaid bills."

DeKok's face creased with concern.

"It's not that I'm sorry for Alia. She made enough in her day. But it *is* a strange situation."

Lowee murmured agreement. Vledder remained quiet, listening intently.

"I done checked widda lot of da guys, but nobody knows wha' hoppen. Alia says they shook him down before they killed 'im. She say it coulda bin a vendetta. Rickie dome make 'isself some enemies."

"Did she mention names?"

Lowee shook his head.

"I only knows she godda few of da guys to 'elp 'er."

"Get revenge?"

Lowee grinned.

"Call it justice."

DeKok drained his glass and waved away a refill.

"Have you any idea in which direction she's looking?"

"Look like," he said carefully, "datta Antwerp is a town with lotsa dealings in glimmers, and Rickie usta do a lot in that business."

DeKok pursed his lips.

"I know Rickie dealt in diamonds, but the business is closed to outsiders, based on trust. You only cheat once in that business and you're simply frozen out. You never make another legal deal." He paused, trying to follow Alia's reasoning. Then he turned back to Lowee.

"Was Rickie in Antwerp often?"

"At least one, two days a week. He brung me a coupla stones sometimes."

DeKok smiled.

"I didn't know you dealt in diamonds."

"If there's green innit, I'm innit."

DeKok yawned and asked Vledder for the time. It was almost midnight. Slowly he lowered himself from the stool.

"Bye, Lowee," he said tiredly. "I'm going to get a few hours sleep."

Lowee raised a hand.

"Wait a sec. Almost forgot." He turned and took a long folder from between some bottles. The cover was overprinted with autumn leaves in glossy red and yellow. The text was in Gothic letters.

"Apache Alia goddit in Rickie's place. She ask me to give it to youse, if I sees you."

The gray sleuth looked at the folder. The tired expression on his face changed to a steel mask as he read the text on the cover.

"Come unto us," he read aloud, "we take care of your death until the funeral."

Below the text, almost at the bottom of the page, was a penciled notation. It was the word "Me" with a question mark.

DeKok pointed it out to Lowee, who nodded.

"That's Rickie's fist, alright."

9

The new day started with a brilliant sun rising from behind Central Station. It turned the ice on the trees into millions of blinding, glistening diamonds.

DeKok looked at it with pleasure. He loved his city. It was an unlimited love that was part of his soul. As far as DeKok was concerned, there was no city in the world that could equal Amsterdam for its beauty. What other city could boast so much beauty, such a diversified population, and...so much crime?

DeKok looked around and grinned to himself. He had to confess he knew few cities outside of Amsterdam. He never had the urge to travel. When he thought about it, he realized he had been to a few other cities and towns in Holland, but had never been abroad. He simply lacked the desire and curiosity. He preferred to be at home, enjoying his wife's culinary achievements, or ambling through the old inner city, where he knew every stone in every street.

He glanced at Vledder, who was behind the wheel. The young inspector looked pale and tired.

"Had a bad night?" he asked, concern in his voice.

"Yes, very bad. I kept waking up."

"Why?"

Vledder was irritated.

"Why?" he snarled. "Because you have the wonderful talent to continually surround a person with new problems."

DeKok looked surprised.

"Me?" he exclaimed, offended. "I don't bring you any problems! I don't confront you with riddles—others do that."

Vledder snorted.

"Why were you so happy when Lowee gave you that folder last night?"

DeKok's eyes held a glint of mischief.

"I was happy?"

Vledder nodded with emphasis.

"I know you. How long have we been partners? You were so happy, so fascinated, as if you had received a gold ingot."

DeKok shrugged.

"I never looked inside. The text on the cover somehow got to me. 'Come unto us,' he quoted, "'we take care of your death until the funeral.'" He looked at his partner. "Doesn't that intrigue you?"

Vledder slowly shook his head.

"Why should it?" he asked contemptuously. "I read it front to back last night. I couldn't discover anything significant. It's a publication from the HPD."

DeKok moved in the seat.

"The HPD?"

"Yes, the Holy Pact of the Dying."

The corners of DeKok's mouth pulled down in a sorrowful expression.

"Does such a group exist?"

Vledder nodded.

"Certainly it exists. Because you seemed to be so fascinated with the folder, I checked before you came to the office."

"And?"

"The HPD is a kind of sect, with unique beliefs. It is independent of any recognized religion. The folder is one of the ways they attract members."

"People preparing to die?"

"No, the idea is to live in anticipation of death."

"I don't understand."

Vledder sighed demonstratively.

"It's not that complicated. One of their people explained it all to me."

"Who explained what? Come on, this is like finding hen's teeth."

"It was a man I reached by telephone. I simply called the number inside the folder. The contact would have preferred a personal interview. When I insisted, he told me the HPD was dedicated to giving people the opportunity to prepare for death, relieved of all worldly concerns and worries. According to my informant, death is too abrupt and too final, always comes unexpectedly and too soon. People generally don't have the time or opportunity to reconcile themselves with God and the world. This group wants to assist in that process."

"A noble goal," said DeKok admiringly. "Their effort deserves support." He glanced aside. "And where is this noble organization located?"

Vledder did not answer. Although Vledder's attention was on the road, DeKok felt he was avoiding the question.

"Where is the HPD located?" repeated DeKok insistently.

The young man gripped the steering wheel tighter. There was a stubborn expression on his face.

"Antwerp," he said finally.

Vledder parked the VW near the fence surrounding Sorrow Field Cemetery. Both inspectors got out and walked in the direction of the chapel.

It was markedly less cold than on their previous visit. There was almost no wind, and the ice thawed on the trees.

DeKok unbuttoned the top of his coat, allowing the cool air to refresh him a bit. When they reached the chapel, they scanned the group of attendees. They spotted Little Lowee, looking out of place, in a group of well-known underworld figures. A little farther away, DeKok recognized a number of aging prostitutes, old acquaintances of Apache Alia. There was also a small group representing the Salvation Army. Their sober uniforms fit in well with the decor.

The same undertaker, in top hat and gray gloves, went from one person to another with the condolence register.

DeKok nudged Vledder.

"Go and ask if you can borrow the book afterward."

Vledder was feeling obstreperous.

"I don't feel much like it," he protested. "It'll just

mean more trouble and more work."

The gray sleuth looked at him for a moment, then stepped resolutely away. With a smile, Vledder stopped him.

"Relax," he mocked, "I'll just wait until his hat blows away."

"There's no wind," DeKok protested.

Vledder laughed.

"I just don't understand," he shrugged, "what you want with that book."

DeKok gestured around.

"I just want to know if there are people here who also attended the Assumburg funeral."

Vledder was taken aback.

"You expect that?"

"Yes."

"Why?"

DeKok looked irked.

"Do I speak Russian?"

Vledder shook his head.

"Apart from the fact that each gentleman found his end in Antwerp, I see no other similarities."

"You forget one important fact."

"Which is?"

"Both gentlemen were well known to be rather comfortable financially. But when death suddenly struck, both were penniless."

Vledder gave DeKok a measuring look.

"Death did not strike suddenly," he corrected. "That's clear from what has been said. They both knew perfectly well death was near."

"That, too, is a point of similarity," nodded DeKok.

A gleaming black hearse crept across the path leading to the chapel. A short distance behind followed the limousines. The doors to the chapel opened, and a flower-bedecked coffin was carried inside.

As before, DeKok and Vledder followed behind the mourners who crowded into the chapel, assuming their place at the back wall. They watched a distinguished man dressed in black take his place behind the lectern. The man arranged some papers and coughed discreetly. Then, in a theatrical gesture, he reached out with both hands to the congregation.

"May God," he said loudly, "give you His blessings and peace. Amen." He lowered his arms and continued more sedately. "And Jesus said, 'I am the resurrection and the life; he that believeth in me, though he were dead, yet shall he live. And whoever liveth and believeth in me shall never die.' Today we take leave of…"

DeKok ignored the scripted words of the minister, focusing his attention on the faces in the crowd. Near the front, like a queen surrounded by her ladies-in-waiting, sat Apache Alia with her strangely attired friends. Right behind her, in the second row, in dark, tight suits, were the delegates of the underworld. DeKok idly wondered how many years of jail time the men had served collectively. After a quick calculation, he concluded it was at least a century.

His musings were suddenly interrupted by the speaker.

"*De mortuis nil nisi bene*," he exclaimed dramatically. "Of the dead…of the dead you will hear me speak no evil. We mortals have not the right to judge his deeds. If his life, by whatever measure, was wrongly lived, he will already have been judged by Him who knows all the facts. We do not know, and will probably never learn these facts." The speaker fell silent for a moment and then leaned forward. After a long look at the audience, he bowed his head. "Let us pray for God's mercy...also for the killer."

While the prayer continued, the inspectors looked at each other.

DeKok nodded.

"Same minister, same speech," he whispered.

Vledder and DeKok strolled back to where they had parked the car. The burial had been uneventful, with the exception of Apache Alia suddenly throwing herself across the coffin, sobbing and screaming.

The Reverend Sijbertsma had continued the tradition and used the same words at the gravesite as he had done a few days before during Assumburg's funeral.

Vledder gauged DeKok's mood.

"Did you see anybody who had risen from the dead?"

DeKok shook his head.

"No, it was just a gathering of the underworld. I've seldom seen such a prize collection all in one place."

Vledder smiled.

"I noticed that Little Lowee seemed to fit in well with the wise guys. I really had the impression he's accepted as one of them."

DeKok nodded.

"That's right," he said resignedly. "And he's my friend."

"What about the minister?"

"You mean the same speech?"

Vledder grinned.

"Is it possible that Rickie, too, asked him to *adorn* the truth?"

DeKok looked thoughtful.

"It's possible," he admitted grudgingly. "I some-times feel anything is possible in this case." He sighed. "Reasonable or not, the reverend didn't say anything about it during our visit."

"But at that time he must already have known that he would be speaking at the funeral."

DeKok nodded.

"Even so, he could not have known we would also be interested in Rickie's funeral." He smiled. "I'm inclined to think that our reverend friend was simply too lazy to write a whole new sermon."

Vledder grimaced.

"So he just blandly repeated the speech he had used for Assumburg?" There was disbelief and doubt in his voice.

DeKok spread wide his hands.

"Why not? I see no problem. The text was appropri-ate. Just the listeners were different." He paused while he thought. "But," he said, "it might be a good idea if you call Sijbertsma later and ask him who approached him to give the sermon." With a grin he pushed his hat forward and scratched the back of his neck. "The cream of the underworld listened solemnly to the words of a Freethinking Dutch Reformed Protestant minister. Believe me, it was worth the price of admission."

Vledder suddenly stood still.

"Antwerp," he said hoarsely. "Perhaps the request came from Antwerp."

"Who in Antwerp?"

"The HPD, of course."

DeKok shook his head in disagreement.

"I don't know, didn't they say in that brochure that they take care of you *until* the funeral?"

10

Vledder started the engine and backed out of the parking place, setting a course for Amstel Dike. DeKok looked around. Near Berlage Bridge an old Rhine barge pushed laboriously through the ice floes. The thaw had suddenly released the Amstel from its icebound isolation.

"You think Henry Assumburg also received a folder from the HPD?" asked Vledder.

DeKok pushed back his hat.

"It seems more important to find out if both were part of the holy pact."

"Surely that can be established."

"Certainly. Perhaps the two were so inspired by the lofty motives of the organization, they freely gave up all their earthly possessions."

Vledder nodded agreement.

"That's not as strange as it sounds," he said, admiration in his voice. "It often happens that dying people deed their possessions to nonprofit organizations. It could be a reasonable explanation why neither Assumburg nor Rickie had a penny left when they died."

DeKok ignored the remarks.

"Did the undertaker promise to deliver the condolence register?" he asked, all business.

The young inspector nodded vaguely. He preferred to avoid the subject.

"Are we going back to the office?"

DeKok shook his head.

"We have an appointment."

"With whom?"

"The director of Ijsselstein Bank."

"What time is it?" asked DeKok as they exited the car. Although he had a watch, he never consulted it. It was one of his many peculiarities.

"Almost a quarter past twelve," said Vledder.

"Well, let's hope the director will receive us. We're almost fifteen minutes late."

"And let's hope he speaks the truth," added Vledder. "The last one lied. Got himself murdered a few days later."

"Yes," said DeKok, remembering an earlier case, "in some countries that would be called justice."

After climbing the wide monumental stairs, they walked through an imposing lobby toward a man behind a white marble counter. The man was dressed in an impeccable dark blue uniform. His blazer had wide silver lapels embellished with the bank's emblem.

DeKok took off his hat.

"We're, eh, Police Inspectors Vledder and DeKok of Warmoes Street station. We have an appointment with Mr. Busenberg."

The man looked at an enormous clock suspended by chains from the ceiling. He flashed the inspectors a haughty look.

"By this time of day," he said in a bored voice, "Mr. Busenberg has gone to lunch."

"In this building?"

"Yes."

DeKok showed his most winning smile.

"Nevertheless, I am certain Mr. Busenberg will be happy to receive us."

The man left the counter with obvious reluctance and disappeared through a high door. After several minutes he came back and led the men to an elevator.

"Second floor," he said wearily. "Mr. Busenberg's secretary expects you."

DeKok made a formal bow.

"Thank you so very much; your amiability knows no bounds."

When the lift doors opened on the second floor, they were greeted by a muscular young woman in a stylish, if severe, business suit with a medium-length skirt. There was a chilly professional smile on her thin lips.

"If the gentlemen will follow me?"

The policemen walked behind her through the long, pink marble corridor.

Vledder nudged DeKok.

"I have a feeling I'm returning to familiar surroundings."

The gray sleuth rubbed the bridge of his nose with a little finger.

"Money and crime," he smirked, "have always been closely connected."

At the end of the hall, the young woman lifted the

handle of a carved oaken door, held it open with an inviting gesture, and then left without a sound.

Mr. Busenberg looked like a friendly, open man. He had light-blond, curly hair and a ready smile on a slightly too-wide mouth. He sat in a seat with a high back behind an immense desk of highly polished dark oak. He rose from his seat, beckoned the inspectors, and offered seats.

After the visitors sat down, Busenberg looked at DeKok.

"I spoke to you yesterday?"

The gray sleuth nodded.

"I telephoned you."

Mr. Busenberg regained his seat and picked up a piece of paper from his desk.

"I'm familiar with the problems you've experienced in the past," he began carefully. "I hope, perhaps in contrast to my predecessor, to offer my cooperation to the police. Obviously anything I say must be within my authority and not contradictory to the interests of our clients. Hence, immediately after your call, I ordered an investigation." He pushed a button on his desk. "Have Jansen come in for a moment." With a winning smile he looked at DeKok and Vledder. "My head cashier," he explained.

DeKok nodded his understanding.

"We need the name of the man who paid out the balance of Mr. Assumburg's account."

Mr. Busenberg made a negating gesture.

"Let us not anticipate each other. It seemed to me better for Jansen to tell you directly, in his own words. It may shock you."

After a light tap the door opened and a balding man entered the room. DeKok estimated him to be in his late fifties. He wore brown trousers and a tweed jacket with leather patches on the elbows.

Mr. Busenberg again came out of his seat.

"These are the gentlemen from the police," he pointed. "They would like to hear from you, personally, about the closing of Mr. Assumburg's account."

The head cashier bowed his head in acknowledgement. He took some papers out of the pocket of his jacket.

"I have copies of the payment. That way you will see we made no mistake in the date."

Busenberg pointed at the papers.

"The police are welcome to the copies...as proof that we acted correctly." He paused while Jansen placed the papers into Vledder's outstretched hand. Then he coughed for attention. "Young Mr. Waal came to see you that day and —"

The head cashier addressed DeKok.

"Mr. Waal is one of our younger associates. He serves the clients at the counter. As you know, we're primarily an investment bank; we do not have a lot of walk-in traffic."

"We know," said DeKok.

"Eh, yes. Well, it was about four o'clock in the afternoon when he told me a certain Mr. Assumburg was at the counter expressing a wish to close his account." Jansen smiled. "We're very possessive of our clients. I mean, we find it unpleasant when a client wants to sever his relations with the bank. Therefore I asked Mr.

Waal to show Mr. Assumburg into my office so I could talk to him. A conversation like that is often revealing, you understand. Sometimes there are small complaints, misunderstandings—"

DeKok interrupted.

"You knew Mr. Assumburg?"

"Certainly."

"Personally?"

Jansen nodded.

"I had often been in a position to advise him on investments. I knew his tendencies. Mr. Assumburg was a man who liked to take a calculated risk, if the potential profits warranted it. I remember the day that the shares of—"

DeKok interrupted again. He was impatient with the long-winded explanations.

"So, he came to your office?"

"Yes."

"And who entered?"

"What do you mean?"

"Who was the man who entered your office?"

"Why, Mr. Assumburg."

DeKok's mouth fell open.

"But that's impossible," he stammered, momentarily loosing his professional composure. "That's impossible," he repeated. This time he was more collected. "At that time Mr. Assumburg was dead…murdered in Antwerp."

The cashier slowly shook his head.

"He was not dead, certainly not. On the contrary, Mr. Assumburg was the picture of health."

DeKok stood up from behind his desk. Slowly he began to walk up and down the detective room in his characteristic ambling gate. He loved doing that. It seemed his thoughts ordered themselves according to the cadence of his pace. And there was, he thought, a lot to sort out. The facts and events of the last few days were so chaotic. There were no obvious connections, no unifying thread. Everything seemed to mock reality…a contradiction to physical laws and commonsense logic. You just don't run into dead people. But that is exactly what had been happening. Despite all the mocking and ridicule, nobody was going to convince him otherwise—he *had* seen the dead Ronald Kruisberg in the cemetery during Henry Assumburg's funeral. He was convinced Mrs. Kruisberg, too, knew her husband was still alive.

But how was that possible? The question persisted. His puritanical soul did not believe in ghosts materializing. He was too sober and skeptical. And what of the appearance of the recently buried Mr. Assumburg?

A long life of crime fighting had created a mildly cynical outlook on life for DeKok. It left little room for the paranormal or occult. His mouth suddenly shaped into an amused smile. He resumed his seat behind his desk. He looked at his younger colleague.

Vledder had spread the bank's papers on his desk and was doing something with his computer. Uploading, or throughputting, or something, thought DeKok. The technical maneuvers were incomprehensible to the gray sleuth. He passively watched Vledder make some keystrokes and saw the papers swallowed by a small, flat machine. As the papers emerged from the back of the machine, Vledder stacked them neatly. One piece of paper, smaller than the rest, he kept aside and stared at. It was the final receipt with Assumburg's signature.

"It's incontrovertible," he mused aloud. "The date is right anyway, February 19. It was the day *after* Assumburg died in Antwerp." He looked at DeKok. "I compared the signature with the samples on record at the bank."

"And?"

Vledder grimaced.

"Real, suspiciously real. And it's certainly not a simple signature to duplicate." He stared at the receipt, then waved it in the air. "Two hundred and fifty thousand euros. What do you think? Would it provide enough incentive to return from the grave?"

DeKok growled.

"Maybe. But would it be enough to bribe St. Peter at the pearly gates?"

Vledder laughed.

"Why would St. Peter want all that money?"

DeKok stared listlessly into the distance.

"Sometimes," he said slowly, "I feel Heaven could do with a little infusion of capital."

Vledder hardly heard him.

"Whoever took the money out of Ijsselstein Bank must have been a master con artist." There was admiration in his voice. "It wouldn't be all that easy to assume a disguise good enough to fool that old, dried-out head cashier. He was convinced he was dealing with the real Assumburg."

DeKok's face fell. His partner's words irritated him.

"You would do well to forget those stupid stereotypes in your thinking," he censured. "If you persist, you'll make some big blunders in the future. Captains of airplanes are not always dapper and brave. Priests are not always meek and patient. Freighter captains are not always drunk. Bank employees are not always old and dried out..." He paused and took a deep breath. "Head Cashier Jansen was alert and careful."

Vledder grinned.

"Not alert enough, otherwise he would have spotted the con."

DeKok's face became expressionless.

"There was no swindle."

Vledder gaped at him.

"No con, eh, no swindle?"

"No."

Vledder waved the receipt in the air.

"You mean..." He did not finish the sentence, confused.

DeKok nodded.

"Jansen paid out the funds to the correct party. He paid Hendrik-Jan Assumburg."

11

Vledder shook his head in despair.

"That's just an assumption...an assumption based on the observations of one man." He gave DeKok a challenging look. "Why could the cashier not have made a mistake? Surely that's possible? Of course Jansen says he paid out to the right person. That's his justification. Otherwise he has to admit he made a huge mistake."

DeKok had a sober look on his face.

"I did not make a mistake," he said calmly, "when I saw a live Ronald Kruisberg at Sorrow Field. Jansen did not make a mistake when he paid out to a live Assumburg."

Vledder banged his fist on the desk.

"But both are dead and buried."

"I don't believe that anymore."

Vledder looked dumbfounded.

"You don't believe it anymore?" he exclaimed fiercely. "We were both at Assumburg's funeral, and I made a neat report for the Antwerp police in which I confirmed the burial."

"And?"

Vledder gesticulated wildly.

"What do you mean *and*? You don't want to suggest I made a false report, do you?"

DeKok shrugged.

"You didn't know any better," he said calmly.

The young inspector snorted loudly. His nostrils flared and his face turned red.

"And I *still* don't know any better," he bristled. "As far as I'm concerned, Assumburg is dead and buried. Dead and buried he remains. Don't ask me to have a hand in bringing him back to life." He pointed at DeKok. "And as far as Kruisberg is concerned…"

Vledder did not complete his sentence. He fixed his attention on a young woman who was at the entrance. She turned to the detective nearest the door who pointed at Vledder and DeKok across the room. Her gaze followed the pointing finger. She turned away from the desk and approached the back of the room.

DeKok studied her as she approached. She was slender. She wore dark slacks and sturdy walking shoes. As she headed in their direction, she removed a fur coat and draped it over her arm. She had shoulder-length wavy blonde hair. Her free hand held the leash of a beautiful dog, a sand-colored German shepherd with a dark-brown back and black snout. The dog looked alert, ears erect, listening for the slightest sound. As the dog flowed nearer, its eyes became restless and the hair on its neck and shoulders rose.

DeKok loved dogs. After the death of his faithful boxer, he'd obtained another dog. DeKok had shamelessly maintained that his first animal looked like him. They were, he said, "as close as twins." Almost inevitably, the second dog, Monty, was another boxer. DeKok again insisted the dog looked just like him. It was not always certain who was the dog and who was the master. There were times when Monty took the lead and, with no need for words, determined what DeKok should or should not be doing.

Now, without fear, DeKok kneeled down next to the dog. Then he looked up at the young woman.

"What's his name?"

"Droes."

"Droes," repeated DeKok and savored the name on his tongue. At the same time he became aware that the young woman was extremely beautiful, lovely. He took in her exquisite oval face. Her ivory skin and almond eyes made an indelible impression. He stroked the dog's head a few times and scratched behind the ears of Droes, who tentatively began to wag his tail.

DeKok stood up and pointed at the chair next to his desk.

"How may I be of service?" he asked politely.

She took the seat and with a gesture made the dog lie down. Then she leaned toward DeKok.

"I'm Jenny...Jenny Klebach. Actually it's von Klebach, but I don't use it. It sounds too German." She tilted her head to one side. "And you are Inspector DeKok?"

DeKok nodded slowly. The attraction that seemed to surround her like an aura disturbed his concentration.

"With a kay-oh-kay," he said automatically.

She smiled tenderly.

"Ronny told me you would react that way."

DeKok was able to concentrate again.

"Who's Ronny?"

"Ronny. Ronald Kruisberg."

DeKok made a gesture in her direction.

"From the old Peat Market, with the view of Mint Tower."

Jenny Klebach smiled again, more broadly. Her mouth opened slightly and two small dimples appeared on her cheeks.

She praised him. "You have a good memory."

DeKok gave her a searching look.

"Did Ronald send you?"

The young woman shook her head resolutely and the dog at her feet lifted its head slightly.

"Ronny doesn't know anything about this," she said sharply. "And I hope he will never find out. He doesn't like it when I, as he says, *mother* him."

DeKok smiled amiably.

"It's a feminine characteristic I admire."

"Ronny doesn't. He becomes very angry whenever I try to protect him."

"And that is necessary?"

"What?"

"That you protect him?"

Jenny nodded slowly to herself.

"I think so. All isn't well with Ronny. Not really. He's almost impossible to live with—it's gotten worse, especially the last few days. He's snarly, nervous, and tense." She bit her lower lip. "And he's more often with his mother than with me."

"In Diemen?"

"Polderland, yes."

"Did something happen?"

Jenny Klebach shook her head.

"Not between Ronny and me."

"Between Ronny and whom?"

For a moment she looked around, a panicky look in her eyes.

"Nobody. It's his mother."

DeKok narrowed his eyes.

"What's the matter with his mother?"

The young woman did not answer. She turned her head away and the German shepherd suddenly stood up, tense and alert.

"What's the matter with his mother?" repeated DeKok, more insistent.

Jenny swallowed.

"Ronny's father died two years ago in a traffic accident, in Antwerp. He was buried here, in Amsterdam. But now his mother keeps saying his father is still alive."

DeKok moved uneasily in his chair. He glanced at Vledder, but the young man had his eyes on his notebook, busily taking notes.

"Where did she get that idea?" asked DeKok.

Only someone who knew him very well, like his wife, could have detected the undertone of tension in his voice. But the dog suddenly looked at him and flattened its ears. Jenny had not noticed anything.

"She says she saw him."

"Where? When?"

"A few days ago, at Sorrow Field during Ronny's uncle's funeral."

"Mr. Assumburg?"

"Yes."

"And is Ronny trying to talk her out of her silly idea?"

She shook her head.

"He believes his mother without question. He even thinks he might have caught a glance of him himself."

"Where?"

"Near our house, on the Peat Market."

DeKok looked doubtful.

"But that's impossible. Dead is dead. There's no way back."

"I said the same thing," nodded Jenny. "But Ronny won't listen. He's rebellious and bitter. Ronny's father seems to have been a, eh, an unpleasant man, to say the least. The very idea he's still alive gives his mother nightmares."

"And Ronny?"

She lowered her head, tears filling her eyes. The dog moved restlessly and put its head on her lap.

"I'm afraid. I'm scared to death."

"Why?"

"For Ronny. He's changed so...I just don't know him anymore. I'm afraid he'll do it for real."

"What?"

"Kill him."

DeKok leaned closer, ignoring the soft warning growl of the dog.

"Kill whom?"

She looked up with a teary face and subconsciously patted the head of the dog.

"His father. He's said several times, 'If he's still alive, I'll personally bash his head in.'"

"You think he means it?"

Jenny Klebach nodded her head, tears rolling down her cheeks.

"I'm afraid so."

After Jenny Klebach and her dog had left, DeKok looked questionably at Vledder.

"Any comment?"

Vledder shook his head.

"Give me a moment. When I take notes, I don't really think about the meaning of what's said. Usually that happens when I transcribe my notes on the computer." He glanced at his notes, then looked up and shook his head ruefully.

"We," he said formally, "will have to accept a live Ronald Kruisberg as a reality."

DeKok laughed out loud.

"We?" he exclaimed, pleasantly surprised. "You were the one who had trouble with it, right? I was convinced the moment I had to give up chasing him at the cemetery. I only wondered at the time how, and if, I could revive the old Spanish Enterprises fraud case."

Vledder grinned sourly.

"Well, if you wait until young Kruisberg kills his father, it will be a homicide case and you'll be free to pursue it to your heart's content."

DeKok's face became serious.

"I approached the family a bit suspiciously in the beginning. I kept thinking the whole Kruisberg thing was a separate case and felt the family was part of it.

When young Kruisberg came to see us, I suspected that old Kruisberg's existence had been common knowledge for some years. It seemed as though I had discovered a secret. *Now* I understand. Ronny just came to verify his, and his mother's, observations."

"What about the threat?"

DeKok stared into the distance.

"I can understand that. But I also hope to catch up with his father before he does. Believe me, I have some searing questions to ask."

"About Spanish Enterprises?"

DeKok nodded.

"Yes indeed, but I'm even more interested in his, eh, his return from the dead. I feel the Kruisberg thing is just part of a much larger picture."

Vledder looked baffled.

"How do you mean?"

The gray sleuth rested both elbows on the desk and leaned forward.

"Let's see if I can recharge your brain," he said affably. "Ronald Kruisberg and Henry Assumburg knew each other—"

"Yes, they met in Antwerp...through some kind of cult," Vledder chimed in. He was scrolling through a file on his computer and read the transcript of the conversation with Mrs. Kruisberg.

DeKok nodded.

"*Exactum*, as Lowee likes to say. Now, can you think of a name for this cult?"

Vledder's eyes widened and he slapped his forehead.

"Of course," he said, "the pact, the Holy Pact for the Dying."

DeKok nodded again.

"I'm not saying it's true, but it *is* food for thought. Even more so because Henry Assumburg, too, seems to have risen from the dead."

Vledder swallowed.

"You mean this, eh, this cult wakens the dead?"

The phone on DeKok's desk rang. Automatically Vledder picked up on his extension and answered. After a few seconds Vledder replaced the receiver.

"It was the watch commander. Little Lowee is downstairs, wishing to see you. He's on his way up."

DeKok glanced at the large clock on the wall.

"A strange time for Lowee," he murmured. Then he looked at Vledder. "Is that possible?" he asked.

"Is what possible?"

"Waking the dead?"

Before the young inspector could answer, Lowee entered the room. With quick steps he approached DeKok and collapsed in the chair next to his desk. DeKok gave him a worried look.

"Lowee, you belong behind your bar."

The barkeep nodded.

"But I hadda come," he panted. "I dint wanna wait for youse to show up."

DeKok grinned.

"It's that serious?"

Lowee nodded.

"I tole youse I mess around wiv glimmers. But I ain't

gotta time to travel aroun', you know. I gotta gedda guy
to take me places. Anyways, dats why I send Fat Tom for
da stuff. 'E know Antwerp. Tonite 'e comes back a bit,
um, upset, looks like 'e's seasick, or somethin'. I seen that
an ax 'im wats goin' on, you knows? And 'e sez 'e's seen
Rickie from Apache Alia. So I makes a joke, you knows,
and sez, inna white shirt wiv wings?"

DeKok listened intently.

"Then what?"

Lowee sighed.

"Den Tom shook me wiv both 'ands and 'e sez: 'I
swear Lowee...on the life of my child.'"

12

Little Lowee looked at DeKok with pity.

"I knows itsa problem for youse," he said sadly. "But I thunk it were impurtent to come tell ya." He rose. "I gotta get back—they's drinkin' all me stock." He grinned. "Bein' friends wiv youse is costin' me enuf."

DeKok smiled fondly.

"God will reward you," he said simply.

After Lowee left, Vledder sank down in his chair, a look of consternation visible on his face.

"What sort of case did we stumble into?" he asked agitatedly. "In the morning we bury a man, complete with a preacher and an elaborate ceremony. On the same day the dead is observed in Antwerp, very much alive."

"Like an old warlock."

"Huh?"

"Or a banshee, a man or a woman with supernatural powers. They were often seen in more than one place at the same time. I know my grandparents in Urk used to believe—"

Vledder dismissed DeKok's musings with a wave of his hand.

"Can Fat Tom be trusted?"

DeKok banished all thoughts of witchcraft.

"Fat Tom has only one child, a little daughter. He's crazy about his girl. If he swears on her life, then…" He did not finish the sentence. "We can take it at face value that he's seen Rickie from Apache Alia." He paused and thought. "It's just too bad he didn't walk over and ask about his health."

It sounded almost comical.

"Yes, well, I can understand Tom sort of fleeing Antwerp in a panic," said Vledder. "He must have thought he'd seen a ghost."

DeKok gave his partner a measuring look.

"Or a banshee?" he asked sarcastically.

Vledder threw his hands up in the air.

"But there has to be an explanation."

"For what?"

"Fat Tom seeing Rickie."

DeKok shrugged.

"What explanation do you want?"

Vledder ran his tongue along his dry lips.

"Okay, now you're saying, eh, you mean Tom saw a real, *live* Rickie?"

"Yes."

Vledder seemed shocked.

"Fair enough. So who did we bury this morning?"

DeKok stared at nothing, a mulish look on his face.

"That question," he said finally, determined, "we will have to have answered."

Commissaris Buitendam looked relaxed. A few days leave had smoothed out some of the worry lines in his face. A faint smile danced around his mouth.

"You wish to order exhumations?" he exclaimed, amused.

DeKok nodded.

"Exhumations," he repeated. "I want to exhume the bodies that are in the graves at Sorrow Field under the names of Ronald Kruisberg, Hendrik-Jan Assumburg, and Richard Strijdbaar."

"Why?"

"Because I suspect the aforementioned gentleman are still alive."

Commissaris Buitendam laughed scornfully.

"The corpses are walking about?" he mocked.

DeKok felt the beginning of anger course through his veins. He pressed the nails of his fingers into the palms of his hands to regain control.

"I was under the impression that request was formulated correctly," he said, outwardly calm. "I do not maintain that the corpses are alive or any such nonsense. There are reasonable grounds to presume the people buried under those names are, in fact, still alive and walking around above ground."

Commissaris Buitendam frowned.

"Didn't we have a similar conversation some time ago?" he asked crossly.

DeKok nodded.

"The day you went on leave."

Buitendam looked pensive.

"That, as I remember, was about a dead man you thought you had seen alive at a cemetery."

DeKok pressed his fingernails deeper into his hands.

"That was Ronald Kruisberg. And I didn't think it. I *saw* him."

The commissaris produced a sour smile.

"And now there are still more dead people making appearances?" he almost jeered.

DeKok managed to maintain his composure.

"Hendrik-Jan Assumburg, a disreputable businessman, and Richard Strijdbaar, a well-known underworld figure. According to official reports, both were murdered in Antwerp and buried in Amsterdam. However the day after his death, Assumburg withdrew the entire balance of his account at Ijsselstein Bank. Richard Strijdbaar was seen yesterday around noon."

"Can you prove that?"

DeKok shrugged.

"I think," he said, carefully, "the head cashier at the bank, who paid the money to Assumburg, will testify. I'm not so sure about Fat Tom."

The commissaris raised his upper lip slightly.

"Who is Fat Tom?"

DeKok sighed deeply. He was always amazed that the commissaris knew so little about the neighborhoods in which the police operated on a daily basis.

"Fat Tom," he explained patiently, "is the man who recognized Richard Strijdbaar—Rickie from Apache Alia—in Antwerp. Tom is an underworld figure who, if approached officially, will probably deny seeing anything. There's nothing to be done about that. Career criminals don't like to go to court, even as witnesses."

For a long time Buitendam stared at the wall.

"Wasn't Kruisberg also killed in Antwerp?"

"In a car accident."

The commissaris spread the long fingers of his slender hands and placed the tips against each other.

"And what sort of indications do you have...concerning his life and well-being?"

"Aside from my own observations, a third party told me yesterday that his wife and son have also seen him alive."

"And will *they* testify?"

DeKok released the tension in his hands, bent his head, and scratched the back of his neck.

"I'm afraid they aren't ready to accept it."

"What won't they accept?"

"The idea that their husband and father is still alive."

The commissaris was taken aback.

"Why would they deny it?"

DeKok took a deep breath and thought before he answered.

"Sometimes death is a real relief, a liberation," he said slowly and absentmindedly. "And that does not always pertain to just the person dying."

"You mean they were *happy* about his death?"

DeKok looked up at his chief.

"I think," he said solemnly, "neither wants a change in the present situation. You understand? I expect no cooperation in proving Kruisberg is still alive—not from the mother, nor from the son. He is dead to them, and they're content with it." He paused, then continued pensively. "All in all I have little chance of obtaining all the evidence we need. Kruisberg, Assumburg, and Strijdbaar will have assumed different identities. If each keeps a low profile, it will be many years before we can make any progress."

Buitendam rubbed his chin.

"Thus exhumation?"

"Yes."

"What do you hope to find?"

DeKok gestured vaguely

"Anything—lead, stones, sand...perhaps even substitute corpses."

Vledder gauged the heated face of DeKok and shook his head in commiseration.

"You did it again?"

"What?"

"You were belligerent to the commissaris."

DeKok nodded sadly and lowered himself with a sigh into his chair.

"Believe me, Dick," he said despondently, "I didn't want any trouble. I honestly did approach him with a firm resolution to keep my temper."

Vledder grinned.

"But you failed...again."

DeKok made an apologetic gesture.

"I couldn't help it. His refusal was so blunt and unmotivated that I lost my patience."

"No exhumation?"

DeKok shook his head.

"He even refused to present the proposal to the judge advocate. According to him, exhumation is un-Christian. The dead should be left in peace, he said. He added that the very idea was so disgusting, offensive, and revolting, it should have no part in our investigational methods."

Vledder was aghast.

"He's crazy."

DeKok grinned.

"I never used the word."

Vledder was getting excited; his face turned red.

"Did you explain everything to him?"

DeKok nodded.

"I was as candid and straightforward as possible. I can't remember a time I've ever been this frank with him." He waved his arms in a helpless gesture. "I feel he has no understanding of the seriousness. He seems to think our work is just one big amusing game of hide-and-seek with life and death."

"Sounds like there will be consequences," Vledder observed.

"You mean for his refusal to order exhumation?"

"No, for playing hide-and-seek with life and death, as you put it."

DeKok pulled out his lower lip and let it plop back. He repeated it several times. Vledder was disgusted, but hid it well this time.

"It would depend upon the motives. Whether it is Kruisberg, Assumburg, or Rickie, I do not know why any of them preferred an official death over an official life. In the end there must have been several interests or considerations influencing the choice they made. Being a corpse is a definitive solution to avoid earthly judges. As I said before, according to the law, prosecution is no longer possible after the death of the suspect."

"Surely that's logical?"

DeKok shook his head.

"One can be honored posthumously, so it should also be possible to punish posthumously."

"Where is the sense in that?"

"Not for the dead—but what about the heirs? Say after the death of the suspect a judge imposes an enormous fine or assumes the possessions of the suspect. The possessions *would* have been inherited by their heirs. That has certain consequences. Just think, what if a Dutch judge were to decide William of Orange obtained his possessions by illegal means back in the sixteenth century? Our entire royal family would have to go on welfare."

Vledder laughed.

"That's silly."

"Maybe. That sort of thing has happened often enough in the past. Recently, too..." He did not complete the sentence. The subject slipped his mind and was replaced with the reality of his investigation. He gave Vledder a meditative look. "Since the commissaris has refused the exhumation, we'll have to get some travel orders."

"For Belgium?"

"Exactly. After all, the official notifications of death originated there."

The phone rang. Vledder picked it up, listened for a few minutes, and paled. DeKok watched him intently. Vledder made some notes as he listened and then replaced the receiver.

"What is it?"

"They found a man floating in the Rokin Canal, near the Peat Market."

DeKok waved the announcement away.

"It's nothing to do with us. That's third district, Lijn-baansgracht station."

Vledder shook his head.

"Young Ronald Kruisberg is there, on the quay. He identified the body as that of his father."

13

DeKok stood on the rounded aft deck of the rusty delivery barge and solemnly watched as two men from the special drown unit fished the corpse from the dark waters. Ice floes complicated their morbid task. Finally they hooked the body and brought it closer to shore. It was only a moment before they brought it up on dry land.

DeKok wiped the sweat off his forehead. After the notification, he had wanted to walk calmly to the Peat Market, but young Vledder could not stand his ambling pace. He rushed along, the increased tempo pushing DeKok to great exertions.

DeKok was still panting a little, and pushed his old hat farther back on his head. He made his way back to the shore while the drown-unit people handed the body over to waiting morgue attendants. Carefully they put the body on a stretcher.

DeKok appeared next to the corpse. He squatted down next to the stretcher. The corpse stank of canal water.

The gray sleuth studied the dead face. It was familiar. The lines were just a little sharper than he remembered. He felt Vledder's hot breath on his neck.

"Is it Kruisberg?"

DeKok nodded slowly. His eyes were now focused on the large gaping wound on the right side of his forehead, just below the hairline. The water had washed the wound clean. A star-shaped breach in the skull was clearly visible.

"Deadly," he stated.

"The wound?"

DeKok did not answer. Next to the stretcher he spotted the feet of a man. He looked up and recognized young Ronald Kruisberg. He had not noticed the young man was at the scene. The son was dressed the same as when he had come to the police station, in a heavy coat with a fur collar.

DeKok rose to his feet, walked toward the young man, and stretched out a hand.

"My condolences on the death of your father," he said.

The young man shook the outstretched hand weakly, without force. He turned his head aside, avoiding the eyes of the inspector.

"It wasn't me," he said softly. "You have to believe me, it wasn't me."

It did not sound very convincing.

DeKok motioned to Vledder.

"Take him to Warmoes Street."

Vledder raised his eyebrows.

"Book him?"

DeKok hesitated a moment. He could just see over the head of the young man. Suddenly a curtain moved on the second floor of a house along the Peat Market. Then he nodded to himself.

"Yes, book him on suspicion of murder."

Dr. Koning stepped through the circle of curious on-lookers. When he came nearer, he lifted his greenish Garibaldi hat in greeting. DeKok noticed the eccentric coroner was dressed in his usual odd way. He wore a cutaway coat, striped pants, a gray vest, and the inevitable chain for his old-fashioned pince-nez. His only concession to the weather seemed to be a pair of knitted woolen mittens.

"I'm sorry you had to wait," said the doctor, "it's not my habit. But the first reports spoke of an ordinary drowning. It was only later we heard it was a murder." He waved at the morgue attendants. "Otherwise I would have caught a ride with them."

DeKok accepted the explanation with a wide smile. He had known the old, eccentric coroner for years and was very fond of him.

"There is not much of a rush," he said resignedly. "I already arrested the probable killer."

The doctor's eyes lit up with wonderment.

"Already? Even you are usually not that quick. Do you have a confession?"

DeKok shook his head.

"No, not yet," he answered. "But considering the place of the murder, motive, and threats on the suspect's part, I think we had reasonable grounds for the arrest."

Dr. Koning shrugged.

"I don't have to teach you your job. You're old and wise enough. But haste makes waste and the first impression is not always the correct one."

It sounded disapproving.

He walked away from DeKok and went over to the corpse. Kneeling, he peered at the head wound intently and then pointed and looked up at DeKok.

"Not a first blow."

The coroner lifted the victim's eyelids and studied the pupils. He unbuttoned the heavy overcoat the corpse wore. Taking off one of his mittens, he felt his way with a bare hand between the clothes of the dead man.

Several minutes later he straightened up with a deep sigh. His old bones creaked. DeKok watched the doctor attentively.

"The man is dead...I presume?"

The question had to be asked. In the Netherlands, no person is officially deceased unless confirmed by a qualified medical practitioner.

Dr. Koning took the handkerchief out of his breast pocket, took off his pince-nez, and began to clean them carefully.

"Dead? Yes, undoubtedly."

It sounded vaguely mocking.

"Anything special?"

The coroner replaced his pince-nez and stowed the handkerchief back in his breast pocket.

"As I said, the most obvious wound was made by the first blow. The first could have been the fatal one, but there were several blows in the same spot."

DeKok nodded to himself.

"Blood must have come from the wound?"

"Indeed, it must have been quite gruesome."

"The weapon?"

The coroner thought about that.

"I think," he said carefully, "it may have been a hammer with a narrow strike surface. There are no widespread cracks. The fractures are rather concentrated. But the autopsy will reveal more details."

DeKok looked pensively at the corpse.

"What else?" he asked after a long silence.

Dr. Koning did not answer at once. He concentrated on replacing his woolen mitten while his gaze was on the face of the dead man. Then he looked up.

"What's your own opinion?"

DeKok made an uncertain gesture.

"I think that the man was, eh, was suddenly attacked here on the Turf Market and then thrown in the water."

The coroner shook his head in disapproval.

"Sloppy," he reprimanded, "a very careless, premature conclusion." He pointed at the corpse. "This man has been dead for at least twenty-four hours; however, he's been in the water less than two hours."

"What?"

The old man nodded mildly.

"The papers in his wallet are still dry."

With a platinum diamond ring, a cheap Japanese wristwatch, some small change, and a black leather wallet in a borrowed plastic bag, DeKok walked back to the Warmoes Street station house.

He had asked a few uniformed constables to search the Peat Market for traces of blood, but wouldn't hold his breath for the result. Anyway, he thought, headquarters will send the usual bunch of crime-scene investigators. In any event he felt comfortable with Dr. Koning's diagnosis. The crime scene was not anywhere near the water. It was just the place the corpse had been dumped.

After the morgue van and the coroner left, DeKok crossed over to the house where he had seen the curtains move. He climbed the stairs to the second floor. The German shepherd greeted him with an unfriendly growl. Jenny Kelbach was equally antagonistic, but allowed him to inspect the rooms. He took a moment to enjoy the view of Mint Tower, then looked for traces of blood. He did not find any. He also did not find any spots that looked as if they had been cleaned recently.

After Dr. Koning's explanation, he had not really expected to find anything in the house. By now he'd concluded the murderer bludgeoned Kruisberg in a place unknown, later transporting the body to the Rokin Canal. The canal just happened to border the Peat Market.

With the plastic bag dangling from his hand, DeKok walked on. As he walked he silently reviewed the facts he knew, and those he suspected.

It could mean, he thought, young Kruisberg was actually not guilty of murdering his father. It could also mean the real killer was aware the son had threatened his father. It could explain why the corpse ended up so close to the house Ronny and Jenny shared—another red herring?

DeKok grinned to himself. It was an expression of sad self-mockery. Like a rookie, he had fallen into the trap. He'd accused young Kruisberg practically without thought.

In an expression of barely suppressed temper, he kicked the wreck of an old bicycle that was leaning against a pole. *Why not throw the wreck in a canal like everybody else?* he thought petulantly.

The crux of the matter was he still understood too little, almost nothing. What had been dead Kruisberg's motives? Why after his official death had he manifested himself so clearly to his wife and son? Did he want to return to his former life or some other life? Who else knew he had not died in Antwerp? Was it one of the people he had defrauded in the past?

He reached Warmoes Street via the Damrak and Old Bridge Alley. Still deep in thought, without greeting the watch commander he climbed the stairs. When he entered the detective room, Vledder hastily walked over to meet him.

"He's crying."

"Who?"

Vledder pointed at the floor.

"Kruisberg's son—I really feel sorry for him. He came along, meek as a lamb to the slaughter. He acted as if we'd already reached a verdict." Vledder paused and grimaced. "It's a pitiful sight to see a big, strong man softly sobbing in his cell."

DeKok looked closely at Vledder.

"Did you say anything to him?"

"About the murder?"

"Yes."

Vledder shook his head.

"No. I intentionally didn't ask him any questions, either. I'd rather leave the interrogation to you."

DeKok nodded. He threw his decrepit old hat at the peg on the wall and missed. With a groan he bent over and retrieved it. Then he took off his overcoat. He walked over to his desk and sat down behind it. He shook out the contents from the plastic bag before him.

Suddenly, with a face distorted by pain, he pushed back his chair and gripped his calves with both hands.

Vledder looked worried.

"Tired feet?"

DeKok sighed deeply and nodded.

"It's happening again," he complained. "I felt it start as I was walking back. It's a hellish pain. Nothing can be done about it; according to the doctors it is psychosomatic."

Vledder smiled.

"I'm not at all surprised."

"What?"

"Your tired feet."

Still nursing his calves, DeKok looked up.

"You mean there's something wrong with my mind?" There was a hint of suspicion in his voice.

Vledder bit his lower lip.

"No, but it always happens when you're up against it. Whenever you feel there is no solution in sight, your legs start hurting."

"Hmpf," growled DeKok.

"Do you really think that Kruisberg Junior killed his father?"

DeKok did not answer. He stopped his rubbing, lowered the legs of his trousers, and pushed his chair closer to the desk. As the pained look subsided from his face, he picked up the leather wallet and opened it.

The coroner had been correct. Only the edges of the papers in the wallet had been dampened by the canal water. Carefully, DeKok separated and unfolded the papers and spread them over his desk.

"Jan Vries," he read out loud.

Vledder studied DeKok's face. He wondered if his remarks had offended the older man. But DeKok's face was already becoming more cheerful. With a relieved sigh, Vledder grabbed a chair, pushed it closer to DeKok's desk, and sat down backwards, his arms on the back of the chair.

"Jan Vries?" he asked.

DeKok nodded.

"That's the name on his papers."

Vledder grinned.

"A nice alias. About half of Holland is called Jan Vries."

DeKok read on.

"This Jan Vries was born in Kerkrade, Limburg. No fixed address. Established residence is at the Heaven's Gate Temple, Burchtgracht, Antwerp."

With a shock Vledder sat up straight.

"Heaven's Gate?" he asked hoarsely. "That's the head-quarters of the Holy Pact for the Dying."

14

Young Ronald Kruisberg looked disheveled. His blond hair stuck out every which way. His eyes were dull. There were dark circles under his eyes. Unshaven stubble draped his face in a veil. He shook his head constantly with short, jerky movements.

"It wasn't me. It wasn't me. It wasn't…"

He repeated the litany over and over.

DeKok stared at him, outwardly unmoved.

"I've never met a perpetrator," he said calmly, "who immediately, cheerfully confessed."

Ronald Kruisberg looked up. His eyes were filled with tears.

"I know you think I'm lying," he said apathetically. "You have every reason to think that way. I don't blame you for it. But it wasn't me. I did not kill him. God knows I—I would not have been able to do it."

"But you threatened it."

The young man nodded.

"I did. I wished him dead. From the bottom of my heart I wished him dead. Alive he could again drown my mother and myself in misery."

"And that's why you wished him dead?"

The young man lowered his head.

"Yes. I wanted him dead...again." He covered his face with his hands. "It was a shock, a terrible experience. When I saw him floating in the canal this morning, I couldn't believe it. I kept telling myself it was a dream, a nightmare."

"But it was real."

The young man sighed deeply.

"It was all too real," he said softly. "Slowly I became aware of the reality. It went through me like a punishment. Perhaps I deserved heavenly punishment for the terrible desire I had for that man's death. I think I must have stared at his body for hours, unable to move."

"Then you called the police?"

Kruisberg shook his head.

"No, Jenny did that."

DeKok narrowed his eyes.

"Jenny?"

"Yes. She became worried because I was gone so long. She saw me from our window, standing at the side of the canal. She figured there was something the matter because I wasn't moving. She came down in her dressing gown. She saw him, but said nothing. Together we watched. Then she said she was going to call the police."

DeKok had listened intently to the tone and the choice of words.

"Why were you standing there?"

The young man looked up, a question in his eyes.

"Why was I standing there?"

"Yes, how did you come to be there, at the side of the canal?"

"I was letting the dog out. I enjoy the dog, but I don't

want to bother others with him. I don't want him to do his business on the sidewalk or the road. Therefore I always walk him along the side of the canal. Plenty of trees, dirt, and even some grass…in the summer, you see."

DeKok nodded, satisfied with the answer. He did the same thing. If he didn't walk the dog in his backyard, he always walked his own dog at the side of the canals, or places where people and children were not likely to come. And he always carried a plastic bag with him in case an accident happened on the pavement.

"When did you first learn that your father was still alive?"

"About a month ago. I was visiting my mother—I found her depressed and upset. She told me my father was alive, she told me she had seen him."

"Then what?"

"At first I didn't believe her. I told her she must have been mistaken, told her he was dead. But she insisted she had seen him in the city, along Kalver Street. She had seen his reflection in a shop window. It scared her so that she dropped her purse. When she picked it up, he was gone."

"It was not a mistake?"

Kruisberg shook his head.

"I suggested that she go back to the city, the same area, at about the same time. She persisted for days. One day she saw him from the back. It was a back, she said, she would recognize out of a thousand. She followed him, followed the back of the man she had seen. Suddenly, as if by intuition, my father turned around—"

"Go on," prompted DeKok. "Did he recognize her?"

"Yes. He walked toward her, and Mother fled in panic, as if pursued by devils. She ran down Kalver Street and ran into a department store. There she lost him." The young man raked his hair with both hands. "From then on I almost never left her alone. I felt I had to protect her. But I was curious as well. I asked how he looked, if he had changed much."

"When did *you* see him for the first time?"

Kruisberg looked at DeKok. A hint of a smile played around his lips, but not his eyes.

"At the same time you did. It was at Sorrow Field, during the funeral of Uncle Henry. I wanted to know why you chased him. That's why I came to your office, and I knew you lied when you told me about the pickpocket."

DeKok bent his head, but he could not suppress a satisfied grin. He quickly wiped the grin off his face before he looked up again.

"Had there been a renewed contact between your father and mother?"

"No."

The answer was unequivocal. It sounded so cold that DeKok's eyes widened in surprise.

"What about between *you* and your father?"

Kruisberg did not answer at once. He pressed both hands together until his knuckles turned white. He took several deep breaths.

"I just talked to him one time," he finally said, softly and pensively. "Late one evening, I was on my way home when he suddenly stepped out of a dark doorway.

I don't know how he found out where I live. He must
have followed me at one time or another. He must have
followed Jenny as well, according to her, one day—"

DeKok stopped him.

"What did he say?"

"You mean the one time I spoke to him?"

"Yes, of course."

The young man closed his eyes, as if to recall the
incident precisely.

"Although I recognized him at once, I asked who he
was. I even managed to get some surprise in my voice.
He said, 'I'm your father, and I want to remain your
father.' And I answered that we, both me and Mother,
didn't want him to be alive."

"And that's the truth?"

"Yes," nodded Kruisberg, "that's it. Mother and I had
decided to completely ignore him, as if he were, in truth,
dead. We did not want any changes in our lives."

DeKok's face became deadly serious.

"You two would prefer a dead husband and father?"

The suspect looked intently at DeKok, weighing the
sarcasm he had heard in his voice.

"A dead husband and a dead father," he nodded,
self-satisfied. "Yes, indeed. We wanted to maintain our
lives, our status quo, if you will. I realize it sounds heart-
less…for an outsider almost incomprehensible. However
it was a well-considered decision."

"How did he react?"

"He became sentimental. He said he had come back
to correct, make good, his errors of the past. He said
he only now realized how good my mother had been

for him. He said he knew how much she had suffered. I told him that certain scars could never be healed. There were thoughts and memories, bitter memories, that could never be wiped out. I asked him to do us both a favor and disappear...as he had done years ago."

"Cold."

"Yes, it was," agreed Ronny Kruisberg. "And apparently he could not accept it. 'Disappear,' he asked, 'die all over again?' I shrugged my shoulders and made it clear his further existence was of no interest to me. Then he changed his tone and said he planned to pick up his life again where he had left off. He also said we, Mother and I, were part of that. He sounded very determined."

DeKok watched him intently.

"What happened then?"

Ronny closed his eyes. His face was pale and the black circles under his eyes seemed to get deeper. There was an inflexible expression on his face.

"I became furious. I felt the blood rise and my temples throb. I felt like I was going to explode. I yelled at him, screamed, told him I was going to call the police if he didn't disappear. He suddenly grinned, a truly evil grin. He said...he said, eh, 'I wouldn't do that if I were you, my son.'"

DeKok was fascinated by the strange conversation. He leaned forward. The tips of his fingers tingled.

"Did he say why you shouldn't inform the police?"

The young man took a deep breath and nodded.

"Yes. When I asked why I shouldn't call the police, he said, 'After me, others, many others, will rise from the dead.' Those were his exact words."

"Really?"

"Yes."

"What next?"

The young man shook his head, clearly exhausted.

"Nothing next; he disappeared in the darkness."

The inspectors met in front of the newly renovated North-South Holland Coffee House. They walked across Station Square and entered the large hall of Central Station. It was busy. Long queues of people waited in front of the ticket windows. Crowds of travelers streamed toward the exits.

DeKok looked around. He knew he was standing in the most crime-ridden part of Amsterdam. Here operated pickpockets whose techniques were as diverse as their nationalities. Robbers, muggers, and other thieves rented luggage lockers to stash stolen loot to show to fences. A lively trade in heroin, cocaine, and other drugs thrived here. Stolen or fake checks went from hand to hand. Addicted prostitutes searched for business. And for those who were tired of it all, upstairs on the platform there was always an onrushing train for a quick getaway.

The gray sleuth made sure his wallet was in a buttoned inner coat pocket. Then he looked at Vledder.

"You have the tickets and the travel order?"

"Yes."

"Where are we going?"

"Platform five."

"Did you let Ronny go last night?"

"Indeed," said Vledder curtly.

"Had a bad night?"

Vledder did not answer. He mounted the escalator in front of DeKok. Searching along the platform, he found an empty compartment in the Paris Express. The train would go to Paris via Antwerp and Brussels.

DeKok waddled after him and took a seat. Trains had fascinated him since he was a five-year-old boy. He had visited a railway station with his father just to look at the trains. Totally enchanted, he had walked up and down the various platforms looking up at the massive steam locomotives.

"Help remind me that we have to stop by Eisenhower Street this week."

Vledder took out his notebook and made a notation.

"Who are we going to see there?"

"Not who, but what."

"All right, what are we going to do there?"

"I need to go to The Train House."

"The Train House?"

DeKok nodded casually.

"They have an engine on order for me."

"What do you want with an engine?"

"Not just an engine, it's a special locomotive. They didn't have any in stock, so they promised to order it for me."

With an expression of disgust, Vledder replaced his notebook in his jacket.

"You play with model trains?"

DeKok made an apologetic gesture.

"I began recently. It has always been a secret desire. Last week my wife told me I needed a new suit. When she told me it would cost 400 to 500 euros, I told her to give me the money."

Vledder looked amused.

"And you bought model trains with the money," he concluded. "What did your wife say when you came home?"

"She asked me if I'd gone crazy."

"And?"

DeKok grinned.

"I said yes."

The train started to move under the glass roof. DeKok looked out the window and decided his beloved Amsterdam looked less enchanting from a train. They passed decaying warehouses and neglected neighborhoods—there was a lot of garbage all along the track. Suddenly he was reminded of the purpose of their trip.

"Did he have anything to say?"

"Who?"

"Ronny Kruisberg."

Vledder shook his head.

"He was glad to be let go and said only that he would give us his full cooperation to help find his father's murderer."

"Did he offer any suggestion as to the direction we should take?"

"No, but he did offer an opinion about his Uncle Henry's murderer."

"Oh, yes?"

Vledder nodded.

"According to Ronny, the distinguished Mr. van

Ravenswood killed his Uncle Henry. It seems Robert Antoine van Ravenswood had a lengthy, intimate relationship with his Aunt Evelyn. He wanted to marry her."

15

With a final screech the train came to a smooth stop at Antwerp Central Station. DeKok and Vledder stiffly made their way to the platform. Vledder looked around.

"Is nobody waiting for us?"

DeKok shook his head.

"I told them not to bother."

"Why?"

"It seemed better to check out the lay of the land by ourselves, for starters. This afternoon, at three, we have an appointment with the chief commissaris of the judicial police." He smiled. "That's when we'll present our credentials."

"Where is that?"

"At the Palace of Justice."

"You know where that is?"

DeKok shrugged.

"I've never been to Antwerp. To my shame I have to admit that this is the first time I've been outside of Holland."

Vledder grinned dubiously.

"You've never been to the bird market? You've never had a *bolleke*?"

DeKok reacted with sadness in his voice.

"For me, the need to travel is practically nonexistent. If the trail in this case had less clearly pointed toward Antwerp, then I would have stayed in my familiar Amsterdam." He paused. "What's a *bolleke*?" he asked.

Vledder laughed out loud.

"The most wonderful beer in a special glass. It puts Lowee's cognac to shame."

DeKok looked stubborn.

"That's quite a claim."

Vledder nodded.

"I can tell you in all confidence that angels brew it, and only the Flemish know how to pour it just right."

"And the Flemish live in Antwerp?"

"Absolutely."

DeKok smirked.

"Then, in a little while, I'll want a...what's it called?"

"A *bolleke*."

Down beautiful marble stairs they descended from the platform level to the entrance hall. Downstairs, DeKok looked with awe at the vaulted glass ceiling that seemed to reach for the sky.

"A railroad station like a cathedral," he exclaimed with admiration. "A rest stop for pilgrims on their way to eternity."

Vledder gave him a puzzled look.

"Who are those pilgrims?" he asked.

DeKok waved enthusiastically around.

"We...all of us...roaming travelers on a racing planet." In a happy, almost exuberant mood, he walked through the large doors to the outside. Vledder followed him without question. The ebullient behavior of his colleague confounded him. He hardly recognized his old mentor.

Outside, DeKok looked back at the building. The designation of the building was written in large letters in both Flemish and French. He could readily understand the Flemish; it seemed a lot like Dutch. Seeing the French words made him suddenly realize that Belgium was a country with two official languages. Sort of like Canada, he mused.

From the station, Keyserlei invited them. It was a broad, festive boulevard that reminded DeKok of pictures he had seen of Paris. To one side, large and dominant like the Empire State Building, he saw the monumental Mercantile Center. At one time, every merchant involved with the shipping business had had offices there. But as the importance and volume of Antwerp Harbor grew, the various businesses had spread out over the city. Now at least one third of the offices were occupied by companies unrelated to the shipping business.

DeKok looked around with admiration. To a man who had wandered almost his entire lifetime through the narrow streets of Amsterdam's inner city, Antwerp was a revelation. Clean, wide streets sported no graffiti.

"A blank wall is a fool's paper," he said, thinking about the graffiti that so plagued Amsterdam.

"Did you say something?" asked Vledder.

DeKok nodded.

"Something my mother used to say," he said. "Although they did not have magic markers or spray paint in the old days, she gave me insights about a lot of things." He paused and gesticulated. "Don't you notice something different?"

Vledder shrugged.

"Little girls in blue sweaters and gray skirts," he said grudgingly. "Orthodox Jews with long beards and black coats."

DeKok shook his head.

"I don't mean that. Look at the store windows...open and enticing. No gates, no shutters, no barricades against criminal violence. The middle class seem to be able to live here in freedom and without fear."

Irritated, Vledder stood still. DeKok's cheerful voice and the implied criticism of their own city bothered him.

"You seem to forget," he said heatedly, "we're here to investigate a series of cold-blooded murders with tentacles reaching as far as Amsterdam."

DeKok did not react. He ambled casually away from Vledder, determined not to have his pleasure spoiled. It was, after all, the first time he had left Holland. Happy, like any tourist, he enjoyed the different sights and sounds of Antwerp. After a short hesitation, Vledder increased his pace to catch up.

"In heaven's name, what are you doing?"

DeKok smiled benignly.

"Exploring Antwerp." He pointed at a building. "And what is this?"

"The old Mercantile Building," said Vledder with a sour face. "But as far as I know, it's no longer used as that."

"It looks more like an old church after a mob smashed all the statues." He pointed to the left, where a raucous noise resonated from a closed space. "And what is that? What's happening there?"

Vledder sighed elaborately.

"It's the Skipper's Exchange. The skippers of the barges still go there to bid on freight."

"Oh," said DeKok.

DeKok looked around and moved into a side street, a rebellious Vledder at his heels. He wandered aimlessly through old streets that seemed to have been transplanted from the Middle Ages. He studied the facades and gables of the old houses, absorbed the charm of the many squares. He finally stopped in front of the dark entrance of a tavern. He looked at his young colleague.

"Are you buying?"

Vledder nodded and led the way.

It was a narrow, intimate, and cozy room. High windows with yellow- and green-stained glass shed a diffused light on rough, heavy trestle tables and benches. DeKok selected a place near the open hearth. Vledder sat down across from him. A well-built young woman approached them with a question in her eyes, and he ordered two *bollekes*.

"How long are we going to be walking around?" Vledder asked DeKok.

"What time is it?"

Vledder sighed, looking at his wristwatch.

"Almost two o'clock."

"Good," said DeKok. "In a little while we'll order a taxi and have ourselves driven to the Palace of Justice."

The woman returned and served dark brown beer in two large, round glasses with a long stem. She placed a bowl of salted peanuts between the two glasses. DeKok looked at her.

"How far is it from here to Burchtgracht?"

"Blood Mountain?"

DeKok reacted confused.

"It's more a temple...Heaven's Gate."

The young woman shook her head. There was a mysterious, secret smile on her full red lips.

"No, not a gate to Heaven...but a road to Hell."

Mr. H. J. M. Opdenbroecke, the small, dapper chief commissaris of the judicial police, Antwerp, nodded. His face was serious.

"I can well understand the reaction of the young woman in the tavern," he said in his juicy Flemish. "It's a typical Red Light District...not as grandiose as your quarter in Amsterdam, but yet—"

DeKok interrupted.

"I haven't seen the name Blood Mountain on any map of Antwerp."

Opdenbroecke smiled.

"It is not an official name, but every true citizen of Antwerp can point you to Blood Mountain." There was a twinkle in his eyes. "Even many of *your* citizens are familiar with the directions."

DeKok laughed.

"Where does the name originate?"

The chief commissaris made an almost imperceptible movement with a shoulder.

"At the top of Blood Mountain there is an ancient slaughterhouse. It is now a museum. In the late Middle Ages, it was the main slaughterhouse serving the city. It was also the headquarters of the butcher guild. The name is possibly associated with the blood of slaughter. More probably the name is much older than the slaughterhouse. Nearby is The Stone, an old fortification, which also served as a prison. The Inquisition used it for in-terrogations and conducted executions on the square in front of the building. You see, since one of the favorite forms of executions in those days was decapitation, a lot of blood was spilled there."

"And thus, Blood Mountain," said Vledder, who often stated the obvious.

"Yes, although it's not a real mountain, more a slight rise in the terrain. I wouldn't even call it a hill. It's really a neighborhood, you see."

"Yes," said Vledder, belaboring the point, "like the Bowery in New York; *bowery* is an old Dutch word for 'orchard.' There's probably not a fruit tree in the entire city!"

Before either could bring up more examples, DeKok diverted their attention to the case.

"Have you ever had any official contact with Holy Pact for the Dying, Chief Commissaris?"

"We know, of course, they're headquartered at Heaven's Gate, Burchtgracht. However the behavior of the members of that sect has never given us reason to take official notice."

DeKok rubbed the back of his head, as if perplexed.

"At your request," he said, "my colleague and I attended the funerals of Messrs. Assumburg and Strijdbaar. Regarding both people, we have indications they may still be alive."

The chief commissaris smiled politely.

"We heard something like that. It seems rather improbable to us. The identification of both victims, from our side, was extremely careful and thorough, no doubt. Nevertheless you have my personal assurance of our complete cooperation with your investigation."

"Thank you, we're most appreciative," answered DeKok. "We hope we won't have to abuse your hospitality." He consulted copies of the reports from Amsterdam. "From your reports we learned that Mr. Strijdbaar's body was recovered from Bonaparte Dock. Is that a harbor basin?"

"Yes."

"And the body of Mr. Assumburg?"

"From the same dock."

"Both were poisoned?"

"Correct."

"What was the initial reason you suspected a crime in the case of each of the two bodies?"

Mr. Opdenbroecke leaned back in his chair.

"In both cases there was trauma to the head. Also in both cases, part of the face had been removed...probably because of the screw of a passing vessel. By order of the investigating judge the bodies were turned over to the laws doctor, the pathologist in Holland. The doctor found trauma was not the cause of death in either case. However he did establish there was no water in the lungs. Therefore, as you know, death was not the result of drowning. Our pathological department works differently from yours in Holland. So, the bodies were transferred to the technical police laboratory for toxicological testing. They came to the conclusion that death had been induced by poisoning."

"What kind of poison?"

"Curare."

DeKok sat up straighter.

"Curare?" he repeated. "Inca arrow poison?"

The chief commissaris nodded.

"The poison used in these murders is a new variation, curarine. It was not procured from South America, but from an ultramodern pharmaceutical factory in Holland." He spread his hands in a resigned gesture. "Its use leads to practically the same result. Paralysis of the muscles of the breathing organs followed quickly by death." He sighed. "I have been told that these days there are doctors who use it for euthanasia."

DeKok thought about it. Curare, curarine...he had never encountered either in his long career. How did this strange, exotic poison fit into the puzzle? Would the discovery of the poison prove to be key evidence? How was he going to use it to prove a case?

"Who discovered the corpses?" DeKok asked suddenly.

"One Johannes van den Bosch, owner and skipper of the motorized freight barge *Stella Maris*."

"Both times?"

"Yes."

"Trustworthy?"

Opdenbroecke smiled.

"He's a Hollander."

DeKok frowned. Suddenly the chief commissaris sat up straight and looked in amazement as DeKok's eyebrows seemed to come alive. Opdenbroecke was convinced that two hairy caterpillars were dancing on DeKok's forehead. Vledder had noticed the sudden interest and quickly turned to DeKok. By that time, however, the incredible phenomenon had subsided and there were just two bushy eyebrows left on DeKok's forehead.

The gray sleuth seemed unaware of the brief consternation he had caused. He was pondering the sly chief commissaris. Was he a worthy opponent or ally? The man was hard to judge. Tentatively he looked up from his notes.

"What, eh, is the location of Bonaparte Dock in relation to Burchtgracht?"

Opdenbroecke did not answer at once. For the first time he showed some hesitation.

"You mean in relation to the Temple at Heaven's Gate?"

"Yes."

"It's just around the corner."

16

The inspectors sat enjoying a coffee on the glassed-in terrace of a cafe situated on a lovely little square. In a friendly but firm manner, DeKok had refused the offer of a police escort. He felt more comfortable with just Vledder at his side.

The coffee was delicious, and DeKok enjoyed the sight of the baroque facade of a church nearby. His gaze drifted to the old city library and from there to the statue of the famous Flemish author and printer Plantin. Plantin was said to have taught his people to read. A small sign at the edge of the fountain around the statue stated "No Drinking Water." DeKok smiled. He was certain the text had nothing to do with the ancient printer.

Vledder interrupted his thoughts.

"What is your plan?"

"How do you mean?"

The young man shook his head disapprovingly.

"We're not on holiday."

DeKok ignored the remark. He searched in a pocket and his hand came out with a business card. A reproduction of a painting was on one side of the card. The other side displayed a name and an address. "The tired and true model," he read out loud.

"Model?" asked Vledder.

DeKok nodded.

"It's a model of a tavern, a wonderful restaurant. According to this card and some of my friends, it's not to be missed...a culinary delight. In short, we're going to get something to eat."

DeKok and Vledder walked from the restaurant toward the Scheldt River. The river's banks formed the port of Antwerp. A ferry from England passed in the middle of the river. A Russian ship was docked along the quay, the Russian flag waving from the stern. The outline of hammer-and-sickle could still be seen under layers of paint on the funnel. To the right they saw a magnificent fortification.

Vledder pointed

"That must be The Stone."

"I presume so."

"Then Blood Mountain won't be far."

They walked in the direction of the old fort. Just past the fortress a number of narrow streets meandered upward at a slight angle and led to a magnificent castle.

DeKok pushed his hat back on his head.

"Something this gorgeous," he murmured in awe, "is just called a slaughterhouse in Antwerp?"

They crossed the street and DeKok studied a street sign.

"Burchtgracht," read DeKok. "This is it."

Carefully, as if they were followed, they entered the street.

"This must have been the moat around the fortress," said Vledder. "*Burcht* means 'fortress' and *gracht* means 'canal,' just as in Dutch."

"Mmm," said DeKok, only partially listening to Vledder.

His attention was riveted on an old building at the corner of a side street. The building looked decrepit and dilapidated. Red bricks showed as bloody scrapes through the disintegrating stucco.

"Hea en's Gate," they read in modern blue letters. The "V" from "Heaven" had disappeared.

Vledder licked his lips.

"This is by no means the Heaven's Gate I've always imagined," he said, disillusioned.

DeKok nodded pensively.

"This is an earthly version; no pearls here."

Vledder grinned without mirth.

"I guess so; there isn't anything heavenly about it."

For a few more seconds they stood and watched, as though uncertain how to proceed. Then DeKok resolutely crossed the street, approached the green entry door, and pulled on the cast-iron bell pull. From somewhere inside the building a heavy bronze bell tolled.

Before the sound had died out, they heard the rattle of chains and bolts. The person behind the door opened it a crack. A bald man in a purple surplice stood in the narrow opening. He gazed at Vledder and DeKok.

"Are you truly fatigued?" the man asked, eyebrows raised.

To hide an involuntary smile, DeKok lowered his head.

"Verily," he said evenly, "verily fatigued and weary."

"Enter, Brothers, outside these walls dying is an ordeal."

Via the portal they entered a large hall with black marble walls. DeKok judged it inadvisable to continue the comedy.

"My name is DeKok, with a kay-oh-kay," he said, all business, "and this is my colleague, Vledder. We're police inspectors from Amsterdam."

The bald man smiled broadly.

"You should not let it concern you," he said condescendingly. "Your profession does not pose insurmountable problems." He placed a hand on DeKok's shoulder. "You, too, are heartily welcome."

DeKok swallowed.

"We're here to make an inquiry," he declared. "We would like to speak to your, eh, your leader."

The man's face brightened.

"Brother Gregorius," he said in a jubilant voice. "Pray, be so kind as to follow me."

He turned and led the way down a long corridor. His open-toed sandals slapped on the marble floor.

At the end of the corridor he stopped in front of a set of imposing double doors and motioned for the inspectors to wait a moment. He opened the right-side door and slipped inside. After a few minutes he returned and bowed.

"Brother Gregorius," he announced solemnly, "is prepared to receive you."

A gray, old man was seated on a thronelike chair. He wore a purple surplice, similar to that of the bald man. There was a gold cord around his waist. A number of less ostentatious chairs stood in a half circle before the throne. With a benign smile, he motioned the men nearer.

"Our Brother Simplicius, a name given to honor his noble simplicity of mind, indicated your visit does not concern any personal solicitation. I understand you are both driven by professional motives."

DeKok made an apologetic gesture.

"We're slaves to right and justice." He paused, studying the old man on the throne. "If we had not come in an official capacity, though, what kind of solicitation could we have made in person?"

"People generally come to express the desire of becoming a member of our Holy Pact."

"The Holy Pact for the Dying?"

The old man's eyes lit up.

"You have heard of us?"

DeKok nodded, his eyes never leaving Brother Gregorius.

"Certainly." He took out the folder with the autumn leaves in yellow and red and held it up. "Encountering this in Amsterdam prompted our official curiosity."

The man on the throne showed amazement.

"A simple brochure?"

"Indeed, a simple brochure, but the text is intriguing. 'Come unto us, we take care of your death until the funeral.'"

Brother Gregorius smiled.

"That is correct. We prefer to go no further. The

burial, or cremation, pertains to earthly concerns. There are those who specialize in such ceremonies. We nurture and accompany the dying until death has occurred."

"You provide hospice services?"

The man in the purple surplice pursed his lips.

"We differ from the concept of the usual hospice care. Our convictions don't conform to prevalent opinion. For us, dying is not an end, but a beginning."

DeKok rubbed his chin.

"I don't understand."

Brother Gregorius sighed.

"Dying commences at birth. What one calls 'life' is, in fact, a path to death. Living is a dying process. We are all mortals…in other words, we're all dying."

DeKok looked sad.

"I'm sorry," he said apologetically, "but I find your opinions rather pessimistic." He waved the brochure. "I think this call to come unto you will fall on deaf ears."

Gregorius raised a finger in the air.

"You are mistaken. If the response stays at the current level, we will soon have to dedicate a second temple." He waved around. "This edifice is rapidly becoming too small." He raised his arms and allowed the wide sleeves of his surplice to slide down, then he brought his arms down and put his hands together. "In these anxious times," he explained further, "most people are so actively engaged in 'living,' they consequently fail to allow themselves the time to concentrate on dying. Reading our brochure is a turning point for many people. It causes them to think…to think about themselves and their existence. In many cases it is a depressing, sobering experience."

DeKok finally sat down. Vledder followed his example. They found that despite the imposing chair of their host, all their heads were almost at the same level.

"You are saying," said DeKok slowly, reopening the conversation, "you mean people discover they are no longer satisfied with their present existence, merely by reading your brochure?"

Gregorius nodded.

"Exactly, they become dissatisfied because they realize they have been thinking wrongly—living is not important, but dying is."

"And you're prepared to help them with that?"

"It is our task," said Brother Gregorius piously, staring at the ceiling. "We want to be helpful, supportive. We want to gather those who are lost, nurture them and accompany them."

"Unto death."

Brother Gregorius lowered his eyes from the ceiling and smiled at DeKok.

"Death is not horrible, fearsome, or revolting; death is the fulfillment of dying."

DeKok pressed his lips together and put the brochure back in his pocket. The distorted, convoluted explanations of Brother Gregorius had not erased the purpose of his visit from his thoughts.

"How long has the Holy Pact existed?"

"A little over seven years."

"And the temple has always been here, on Blood Mountain?"

"Our first haven was in Kerkrade, in Holland, but it

did not last very long. We decided our objectives could be better served in a harbor city."

"And the choice was Antwerp."

"Precisely. We considered Amsterdam, but there is little faith left in that city of sin."

"Did you originate the Holy Pact?"

Brother Gregorius sadly shook his head.

"The founder was Paulus Verhoeven, a worthy, noble man. Paulus Verhoeven found that love for one's fellow man should not be a platitude."

"Is he still alive?"

"No. He fell into a ravine during a vacation in Switzerland. He did not survive the accident."

"When was that?"

"Five years ago."

"And you continue his work?"

Their host folded his hands in an attitude of prayer and bowed his head briefly.

"Yes, humbly, in the spirit of our founder."

DeKok resisted the urge to say 'Amen;' instead he rubbed the bridge of his nose with his little finger.

"How do you finance your temple?"

"We receive donations...donations from the dying."

"How much," asked DeKok casually, "was the donation of Mr. Strijdbaar?"

Brother Gregorius smiled delicately.

"Brother Sodomius, we called him that because of his activities in Amsterdam's Red Light District, was very generous. He has assured the continuance of our temple for a long time to come."

DeKok felt his heartbeat rise. The unctuous, at times condescending, tone of the brother irritated him.

"Brother Sodomius was murdered," he said sharply.

Brother Gregorius nodded calmly.

"And that is why you have come all this distance?"

"Among other reasons."

The man seemed surprised.

"I was under the impression the Belgian judicial police had successfully concluded the matter."

"Successful?" snarled DeKok. "For whom?"

"Brother Sodomius. I understand that his funeral was very respectful and in good taste."

DeKok desperately tried to control his mounting anger. He failed.

"Brother Sodomius," he asserted wildly, "was here in Antwerp, at the very moment he was supposedly being buried."

Brother Gregorius looked at DeKok with an oily, insincere smile on his thin lips.

17

Vledder laughed out loud as they walked away from Burchtgracht.

"He was ahead of you, on all fronts and on all points. The way in which he mocked your suggestion that Assumburg and Rickie are still alive was very subtle. He never looked shocked. On the contrary, he remained calm, reasonable. He appeared not to take you, or your ideas, very seriously."

DeKok looked angry.

"And you enjoyed that?"

The young inspector shook his head.

"Not really. But if Brother Gregorius is connected to this case, we have a dangerous enemy."

"Somebody we'll have to take seriously?"

Vledder nodded earnestly.

"It won't be easy to penetrate the temple. Gregorius feels completely safe and secure—with reason." He made a frustrated gesture. "What kind of proof do we have? For that matter, what do we suspect? What do we have to go on? We have a brochure Rickie apparently once had in his possession. We know for a fact Kruisberg, under his alias as Vries, picked the temple as his residence. That's just about all we have."

DeKok stood still, his legs spread. His face was a steel mask. With a gesture of barely controlled anger he raised three fingers in the air.

"Three," he hissed. "Three men—Kruisberg, Assumburg, and Rickie—lived here. These three were members of the so-called Holy Pact for the Dying. All three died and have been observed alive." He took a deep breath. "Perhaps we do not yet have any evidence related to those facts. Maybe even the most stupid lawyer will laugh us right out of a courtroom. However, you can be sure of one thing, whether Brother Gregorius is or is not dangerous, I *will* unlock Heaven's Gate!"

Vledder solemnly nodded and motioned for them to continue on, knowing better than to push DeKok's temper.

Down the street they passed a few aged prostitutes behind curtains. But the activity in the neighborhood did not compare with the constant stream of visitors to Amsterdam's Red Light District.

On a corner they saw a corpulent man in the door of a cafe.

DeKok ambled toward him.

"Perhaps you can help us?" he asked politely. "We're looking for a temple…Heaven's Gate."

"You're a Hollander, aren't you?" asked the man in Flemish. The Belgians and especially the Flemish always referred to the Netherlands as Holland. In the French-speaking part they spoke of *Hollande* and never *Le Pays-Bas*.

"Yes," said DeKok.

The man pointed in the direction from which they had come.

"You must have passed it, back there," the man said, suddenly switching to formal Dutch.

DeKok smiled.

"We did not notice it." He hesitated a moment. "Does the temple have a lot of visitors?"

The fat man nodded.

"People constantly come and go. Sometimes it looks like Central Station. Tramps, homeless, addicts— everybody is welcome there."

Vledder noticed that in all the formal Dutch, the word station was pronounced the Flemish way. The man had said *stasie*, pronounced as "staaahsee." It sounded pleasant and familiar to Vledder's ears.

DeKok smiled.

"And what if one does not belong to those, eh, categories you named?"

The man gave the inspectors a long searching look. Then he shrugged.

"That doesn't bother the brothers," he said nonchalantly. "They are devoted to charity. They feed the hungry and quench the thirst of those in need."

DeKok bowed his thanks and walked back in the direction the man had pointed out.

Vledder grinned.

"I'm afraid we'll have to reconsider our opinion of Brother Gregorius."

DeKok did not react. When they were out of sight of the man in the cafe, they took a side street and set a course for the Great Market.

Vledder snorted.

"I can't say Antwerp has helped us much," he said

somberly.

DeKok looked around.

"We'll find a hotel for the night."

"Tomorrow we're going back to Amsterdam?"

DeKok nodded.

"First thing tomorrow morning please go see the chief commissaris. Ask what he knows about Paulus Verhoeven, who died five years ago in Switzerland. We'll meet up again at Central Station."

Vledder looked suspicious.

"And what about you?"

The gray sleuth shrugged.

"Me? I'm going back to the Skipper's Exchange."

DeKok was not the type of man who was immediately at home in a strange place. For some reason he felt differently about Antwerp. With the confidence of someone who had lived in the city for years, he walked across the Great Market, passed the town hall, and admired the facades of the old guild houses.

Without consciously thinking about it, he found his way to the Skipper's Exchange and entered the building. It was busy, smoke filled, and loud. In the center of the large space a few skippers were seated at long trestle tables. Their faces were weather beaten, and almost all smoked pipes. From time to time they would look at the large blackboards around the wall, where chalked messages about freight and destinations were continually updated. The atmosphere was that of an auction, but there was no auctioneer.

Along the walls were high, narrow Gothic benches that looked antique and uncomfortable.

A man approached DeKok from behind a counter. He had a big stomach barely contained by a yellow t-shirt. He gave the Amsterdammer a long, searching look.

"What ship?" he asked suspiciously.

DeKok grinned broadly.

"The ship of state," he said mockingly. "We carry a lot of freight, but not much of it is going anywhere." He paused and studied the crestfallen face of the man and changed his tone of voice.

"The skipper of the *Stella Maris*," he said. "Does he come here?"

The man nodded affirmatively.

"Certainly," he said, switching to formal Dutch, having identified DeKok as a Hollander. He turned around and pointed at a silent, lonely figure on one of the uncomfortable benches along the wall. "He's sitting right over there."

DeKok thanked the man, then walked over to the seated skipper. He sat down next to the object of his visit.

"Johannes van den Bosch?" he asked softly.

The man raised his eyebrows slightly.

"Van den Bosch, yes, that's me."

"Dutchman?"

The skipper looked a question.

"Would that be a recommendation?"

The gray sleuth smiled.

"My name is DeKok, with a kay-oh-kay. I'm a police inspector, connected to Warmoes Street station in

Amsterdam."

"You're a long way from home."

DeKok made a helpless gesture.

"I'm officially involved with two murders that happened here in Antwerp. According to my information, you discovered both corpses."

"That's right, they were floating in the basin."

"I presume you have given the local authorities all the pertinent information?"

"Of course."

DeKok hesitated for a moment; the bench, with its narrow seat and vertical back, was exceedingly uncomfortable.

"Could there be something, eh, something you might say in retrospect, that was a bit unusual?"

The skipper shrugged his shoulders.

"The bodies were a bit high in the water. When drowned people surface, usually no more than the top of the head is visible. Corpses usually float just below the surface. But with these corpses, the backs, too, were above the water."

DeKok nodded his understanding.

"With a regular drowning no air remains in the lungs as a rule. But there was air in the lungs of these two individuals. They weren't drowned, they were poisoned. They were dead before they hit the water."

Van den Bosch stared at the opposite wall.

"There was something," he said slowly, "I didn't realize until much later."

DeKok moved on the bench. The skipper seemed immune to the uncomfortable seat.

"What was that?" prompted the inspector.

"About two or three days passed between the discovery of the corpses. Both times there was a Dutch yacht in the harbor, at the Bonaparte Dock."

"And not during the days in between?"

"No."

"Do you remember the name of the yacht?"

"It was the *Vita Nova*. I'm always interested in seagoing yachts. It's a kind of hobby. A few months ago the yacht was in Six Harbor, in Amsterdam. I remember admiring her for a while. She's a beauty."

DeKok held his breath.

"Do you know the name of the owner?"

Van den Bosch nodded slowly.

"A certain Assumburg, but I've no idea who that might be."

The train left smoothly from Antwerp Central Station. DeKok leaned back and stared at the houses that slipped by. He slipped into a melancholy mood. In a few hours, the gray sleuth had come to love the city. He knew one day he would be back. Perhaps he would cleanse a robber's nest. In any event, he'd certainly like to walk once again through the silent squares and the sixteenth-century streets. He'd also enjoy another *bolleke* in a narrow tavern with leaded stained-glass windows.

Vledder disrupted his reflections.

"Chief Commissaris Opdenbroecke asked if we had achieved anything."

"What did you tell him?"

"The truth. I said, in fact, Brother Gregorius humiliated us."

DeKok turned his gaze away from the window and looked at his partner.

"Is that the way you feel about it?"

"A bit, yes."

DeKok shrugged.

"He was very courteous and kind. I cannot say otherwise. Apart from that, we'll have to prove, find *solid* evidence, that this temple is no more than a front for nefarious activities." He scratched the back of his neck. "This morning I also had an interesting meeting," he said, changing the subject.

"Oh, yes?"

"Yes, with the skipper of the *Stella Maris.*"

"Where?"

"At the Skipper's Exchange."

Vledder laughed.

"You said you wanted to go back there."

DeKok nodded complacently.

"It was worth the effort. Skipper van den Bosch has an eye for seagoing yachts."

"And?"

"Twice he has seen a beautiful yacht in Bonaparte Dock. Soon after each sighting he found a floating corpse next to his barge."

Vledder's eyes widened.

"Why didn't the Belgian police tell us about that?"

Opdenbroecke didn't know...he still doesn't know. It's a detail the skipper only realized later."

"Can we trace that yacht?"

DeKok smiled.

"It shouldn't be too difficult. It's a Dutch yacht, the *Vita Nova*. Van den Bosch knew the yacht and even knew the name of the owner." He paused for effect. "The owner is a certain Mr. Assumburg."

Vledder almost fell out of his seat.

"What?" he exclaimed.

"Skipper van den Bosh had seen the yacht a few months earlier in Six Harbor in Amsterdam."

Vledder looked pensively out of the window, not really seeing anything.

"It could fit," he said eventually. "Assumburg *did* have a seaworthy yacht. Van Ravenswood told us about it when he came to file a complaint for fraud and forgery."

DeKok rubbed a flat hand over his face.

"On the way back to the train station," he sighed, "I've been wondering how to fit this new development into the whole. I can't yet figure it out. Who was in command of the yacht? Was it a dead, newly arisen Assumburg...or was it someone else?"

The train approached the Dutch border at high speed. For awhile both men were silent, lost in thought. As they crossed back into Dutch territory, Vledder looked up.

"Should we inform the Belgian judicial police?"

DeKok nodded.

"Certainly—we cannot keep this to ourselves. By the way, what did the chief commissaris tell you about Paulus Verhoeven?"

Vledder grinned.

"He must have been quite a character. The police

were glad to be rid of him."

"How's that?"

"Paulus Verhoeven had a habit of starting all sorts of sects, cults, and organizations. He founded Youth for Peace, The Saints of the Last Supper, Back to Simplicity—"

DeKok interrupted the summing up.

"And the Holy Pact for the Dying."

"Yes."

"It seems he was a man of imagination."

Vledder nodded.

"And he always seemed to be able to convince people of his absurd notions. When they became enthusiastic enough, he had them collect money, giving them meager room and board in return for long hours of hard work. As in many cults, some people donated all their worldly possessions."

DeKok grinned.

"So Verhoeven could live it up."

"Exactly. When the police were too close on his heels, he fled to Switzerland with all his liquid assets."

"And, ultimately, fell into a ravine near St. Moritz."

"Yep."

DeKok rubbed the bridge of his nose with his little finger.

"Do you remember where in Switzerland Aunt Evelyn met Assumburg?"

Vledder slapped his forehead.

"Of course, also in St. Moritz."

18

A desultory, depressing rain descended from a low cloud cover. It became so persistent that it looked as if it would never go away, leaving Amsterdam forever shrouded in rain.

DeKok pulled up his collar and pushed his dilapidated hat farther down on his forehead. He ambled in his typical disjointed gait along the gravel path of the cemetery. Water dripped from his face.

Kruisberg Senior was again going to be buried at Sorrow Field. DeKok felt he should be there. It was a question of piety, as well as respect for the living and the dead—two concepts that he believed should not be mocked by mortal human beings.

Vledder positively refused to accompany him.

"I just don't feel like it," he said. "We've been to Sorrow Field twice, both times for nothing. I don't want to waste time again."

DeKok understood, so he did not insist. Silently he left and commandeered a patrol car to drive him to the cemetery.

Sorrow Field looked especially sad and desolate. There were no colors. Even the birds had sought shelter. DeKok ambled on, his head bowed. When he looked up, he saw a man in the distance. He was waiting under an overhang of the chapel. When DeKok came closer, a smile of recognition played around his lips.

"Ronny," he said, pleasantly surprised, "are you the only one here?"

Young Kruisberg nodded, a grave look on his face.

"Nobody else wanted to come. Mother didn't. Aunt Evelyn wouldn't. Jenny stayed home as well. 'For me,' she said, 'your father never lived. He's been dead for years...dead and buried.'"

DeKok looked at him sharply.

"And what about you, Ronny? When did your father die for you?"

The young man closed his eyes for a moment.

"At the moment," he said softly, "I saw him dead in the canal. That's when I realized, for the first time, there was a bond between us. It was a strange feeling; it was both confusing and paralyzing, a mixture of sadness, connection, and guilt."

"Guilt?" queried DeKok.

Ronny nodded.

"Perhaps not guilt in the conventional way you mean. I wasn't the one who took a weapon in his hands, the one who actually administered the blow."

DeKok smiled kindly.

"So, what causes your guilt?"

Ronny sighed deeply.

"I've been thinking a lot about everything for the last few days and nights. A lot happened in a short period of time. I think I became more adult. I grew up enough to know my mother and I have done my father an injustice.

We should have accepted his return. I mean, his return from the dead. Instead of fear of the past, we should have shown courage and strength for the future. We lacked trust. Not just trust in my father, but trust in ourselves. We couldn't trust in the possibility of starting a new life." Sadly he shook his head. "We never gave him a chance."

DeKok's face was expressionless.

"His murderer didn't give him a chance either."

A hearse approached at a disrespectful speed. Near the chapel the car stopped. The wide tires skidded slightly on the gravel. A man stepped out and approached them at a run. He pointed over his shoulder.

"You're here for Mr. Kruisberg?"

They nodded.

"Oh," said the man, visibly disappointed. "You may follow us."

He ran back through the rain. He got into the car and the hearse moved off at a slow pace.

Ronny Kruisberg and DeKok followed on foot. Silently they walked side by side. The shiny black car led the way. The exhaust stank.

The path to the grave was long. The rain came down without pity, soaking the two men. DeKok once again wiped the water from his face.

"I have a strange profession," he began carefully, "full of contradictions. One would expect there to be no room in our job for lying and cheating," he gestured sadly. "But, sometimes, it's unavoidable."

For a while they walked on in silence.

"You told my partner," DeKok began again, "you were prepared to give us your full cooperation."

Ronny nodded as he looked aside at DeKok.

"Yes, I said that."

"And did you mean it?"

"Absolutely."

"Even if there are, eh, certain risks involved?"

The young man nodded again.

"Even then."

DeKok slowed down. The stink of the exhaust bothered him.

"In that case I would like to ask you," he said, "to say something to people around you, people you see rather often. Tell them, in confidence, that the day after his death you received a letter from your father, a letter he must have mailed shortly before he died."

"A letter?"

DeKok nodded slowly.

"A letter," he continued slowly, "wherein your father wrote a list of names, names of people who, like him, have come back from the dead."

"And then what?"

The gray sleuth looked aside.

"I expect somebody will soon contact you."

Young Kruisberg pointed at the hearse.

"His murderer?"

DeKok tilted his head back and allowed the rain to hit him full in the face.

"Not just his murderer," he said solemnly.

"How was the funeral?"

"Depressing—we got soaked."

"Lots of people?"

"Only Ronny was there to bury his father."

"Nobody else?"

DeKok shook his head.

"What, no undertaker...no condolence register?" It sounded cynical.

Vledder pushed aside the keyboard of his computer and leaned closer to DeKok.

"Commissaris Buitendam asked for you. He said the judge advocate is contemplating ordering an exhumation."

DeKok grinned.

"He'll have no choice. Frankly I was surprised that the management of Sorrow Field agreed to bury the same man for the second time."

Vledder nodded pensively.

"This is going to be a mess. Who's in the first grave?"

DeKok snorted.

"Who's in Assumburg's grave? And if Rickie isn't dead, then who's in his grave?" He shrugged his shoulders. "They are, of course, intriguing questions. To tell the truth, I've lost interest in the exhumations."

"But you wanted them," said Vledder, confused. "You fought for them. Were you not extremely rattled when Buitendam didn't approve?"

DeKok nodded.

"That was then, this is now," he said, unperturbed. "I didn't see the pattern then. I just thought it was an intolerable situation to have people popping up who were supposed to be dead."

Vledder shook his head.

"And now? Now you know the pattern?"

DeKok evaded.

"Ronald Kruisberg," he began, "lost his life in a car accident. We have no details; however, chances are the incident ended with an explosion and a fire, which mutilated the corpse extensively. Assumburg and Rickie were both found floating at Bonaparte Dock. Although poisoned with curarine before they hit the water, part of each man's face was knocked away by the screw of a passing vessel. This is according to the Belgian police." He paused and shook his head. "The judicial police in Antwerp aren't fools, and the Belgian investigating judge does *not* release a corpse if that corpse, in his opinion, has been insufficiently identified. In effect, their methods are not very different from ours. When we find a corpse somewhere, we try to identify it. Note this well, we *try* to identify, in so far as possible."

Vledder leaned closer.

"You mean that if a corpse has been mutilated to the extent that positive identification is problematic, neither friends nor relatives are asked to identify the remains. The police must use other methods of identification."

"Such as?"

"Sometimes we find papers, identity papers, on a corpse."

"Exactly what happened with these two victims?"

Vledder sat back with a satisfied smile on his face.

"Now I understand why you're no longer interested in the exhumations. If there are corpses in the graves, they will be so mutilated that they'll be useless for our purposes as well."

DeKok gave his partner an approving look.

"Very good."

DeKok's phone rang. Vledder picked it up and listened. Then he handed the receiver to DeKok.

"It's for you."

DeKok accepted the instrument with a distasteful look. His face fell.

"Already?" he asked hoarsely. "Follow up. And, for heaven's sake, be careful. Be very careful."

19

DeKok walked up and down the detective room with wide strides, markedly different from his usual relaxed strides. He was tired, nervous, and apprehensive. The tenseness reverberated in his diaphragm and caused a queasy feeling in his stomach.

Nothing must go wrong. Nothing. A slight miscalculation, a minute misunderstanding, the slightest glitch in the execution of the plan could all be fatal. The worst part was he could not completely protect Ronny Kruisberg. The murderer had chosen a spot without sufficient possibilities for cover. In his mind he went again over the telephone message from the murderer.

"Come tonight to the tip of Stonehead Pier and bring the letter. You know my price. I will pay you. Don't try to deceive me. If I find out you've made copies, you'll get what your father got."

Young Kruisberg had taped the conversation on his answering machine. It was a crackling, obviously disguised voice, without a detectable accent. Even Ronny had been unable to recognize the voice. Vledder and DeKok listened to an enhanced version of the tape. After several repetitions, each drew a blank regarding the identity of the caller. The original tape had been transmitted by telephone, contributing to the problem. They played the enhanced version to Ronny, again via telephone. Ronny, too, remained at a loss.

DeKok didn't want to risk making personal contact with young Kruisberg. He thought it likely the young man was being followed or was under surveillance. He had not seen him since the meeting at the cemetery. Vledder had made the necessary contacts by phone. He was terse and to the point.

DeKok stood still and looked at the large clock on the wall of the detective room. A quarter past nine. Time was pressing.

The old inspector was familiar with Stonehead Pier. It was a long stretch of dam that stuck out into the River Ij. Warships from foreign nations would usually tie up there during courtesy visits.

The wide dam was closed off with a fence. There was an iron gate where the dam attached to the land. It was the only way to enter the dam from the city. Ronny had to pass through the gate, and after that it would be nearly impossible to follow him unobserved.

DeKok stopped again to think. He rubbed a flat hand over his face again. He wondered how he could have done it. How could he morally justify using the young man for this purpose? What was more important: Ronny's life or the apprehension of a murderer who, DeKok was convinced, would certainly continue his lugubrious activities?

The old man shook his head. It made no sense to abort the mission at the eleventh hour. Near his desk were Fred Prins and Appie Keizer. Although not part of homicide,

Fred and Appie had volunteered their services. DeKok preferred to work with the personnel in Warmoes Street station. He did not like to request homicide personnel from other stations, or from headquarters. Fred Prins was big and strong. Appie Keizer could disguise himself to look like anyone, except a policeman.

DeKok beckoned Vledder.

"Are you going on the boat from the river police?"

Vledder nodded, well aware that DeKok was just asking out of nervousness. Everything was orchestrated. They'd organized, rehearsed, and planned. Nonetheless he answered the question in a casual tone.

"Yes, the boat is a fast one. We'll be close to the dam, with the lights off. We'll only appear when you give us the signal."

Again the old inspector looked at the clock.

"The moment Ronny calls, we'll take our posts."

Vledder said nothing, but merely nodded. That was part of the plan as well.

DeKok was crouched behind a large mooring post just below the surface of the pier. In the distance lights twinkled across the water, but Stonehead Pier itself was shrouded in darkness. The sounds of the city only reached him as a faraway murmur.

If he raised himself slightly, DeKok had a reasonable view of the tip of the dam. Fred Prins, he knew, was hidden across the dam in a similar position. Near the gate, Appie Keizer, looking like a derelict, stumbled drunkenly along the fence.

Ronny Kruisberg stood near the tip of the pier. His silhouette was clearly visible against the lights from across the river. Every once in a while he would stamp his feet and walk back and forth.

It was close to eleven o'clock. DeKok wondered from which direction the murderer would appear. There were not many possibilities.

He felt his tension increase. But the vibration had left his diaphragm and was now in his legs. He was wound up like a racehorse in the starting gate.

Suddenly a beautiful white yacht pierced the shreds of vapor that hung over the water. The yacht turned inland, coming alongside the dam near Ronny Kruisberg, its bow pointing at the river. DeKok could easily read *Vita Nova* on the stern.

A voice from the yacht yelled "Jump!"

DeKok immediately realized the danger. If the young man were to jump, the team would be unable to protect him. He came upright from his place of concealment and yelled at the top of his voice.

"Stand still! Don't jump!"

His yell caused confusion. Engine noise increased and the yacht gathered speed.

DeKok grabbed Ronny and held him. He felt the young man shake. To his right he heard running footsteps. Fred Prins had also emerged and was running to the tip of Stonehead Pier. He made a powerful jump at the last possible moment and landed on the aft deck of the yacht.

DeKok grabbed his flashlight and waved it wildly over his head. Within seconds a gray shadow emerged from the darkness and came alongside.

DeKok released Ronny and jumped aboard the river police boat.

"Follow the yacht," he roared.

All the lights aboard came on, including red and blue rotating lights on the top of the wheelhouse. The siren drowned out the sudden roar of the engines. DeKok almost lost his footing as the boat rapidly accelerated.

Vledder came from the lee of the wheelhouse and helped steady the old man.

"Did you see anybody?" asked Vledder while he picked up DeKok's hat from the deck.

DeKok shook his head.

"Only heard a voice, couldn't see anybody. It was all too quick." He pointed at the light mist across the water. "Fred Prins got aboard."

"Fred? How?"

"He jumped aboard as the yacht was leaving."

"Did he land okay?"

"I think so."

A gust of wind cleared the shred of fog for a moment. Suddenly the yacht was in sight. It seemed to be afloat, but rudderless.

Within moments the police boat was alongside. River police personnel fastened the two vessels together. At that instant Fred Prins emerged from the superstructure of the yacht. He limped a little and there was blood on his face. He looked at DeKok with a grin and pointed a thumb over his shoulder.

"He tried to hit me with a hammer, so I had to knock him out."

DeKok stepped over on the yacht and took a close look at Fred's head.

"Doesn't look too bad, the skull seems intact. You may need a few stitches, though."

A river policeman caught up with DeKok.

"We have a medic aboard," he said to Fred. "Do you need help getting across?"

"No thanks," said Fred, and he climbed the railings to the police boat.

DeKok reached the door to the superstructure and walked forward to the wheelhouse, Vledder close behind.

On the floor, in the shadow of a table, was an unconscious man on his stomach. DeKok pulled the body into the light and then turned him on his back to look at the face.

"Robert Antoine van Ravenswood," panted Vledder.

20

They were all seated in the pleasant, cozy living room of DeKok's house, comfortably sprawled in easy chairs. The gray sleuth lifted a bottle in the air and tapped the label.

Vledder laughed.

"I can't read the label from here, but I bet it's a fine cognac."

"Yes, a present from Little Lowee. He dropped it off this week."

Vledder was surprised.

"Why would he do that?"

DeKok made a vague gesture.

"According to Lowee, it's a celebration. It's been exactly twenty-five years since I visited his, eh, his establishment for the first time."

"Is that right?"

DeKok grinned.

"I don't know, but I believe Lowee."

He poured the cognac into large snifters. The first glass he handed to Fred Prins. The young inspector was still a bit pale. His forehead was covered by a large bandage.

"How do you feel, Fred?" asked DeKok, concern in his voice.

"A lot better," answered Fred. "Apparently I had a slight concussion. Sometimes I'm still a bit light-headed." He felt his head. "Ann sends her greetings. You know what she calls you?"

"No."

"A dangerous old man."

DeKok laughed. He knew Fred's tiny Irish wife. He had met her several times and understood her. It wasn't the first time her young husband had been in harm's way because of one of DeKok's plans. DeKok shrugged.

"But I didn't tell you to jump aboard that yacht."

Fred Prins looked shocked.

"And what would you have had me do? Let that killer just sail away?"

DeKok shook his head.

"I'm truly grateful," he said sincerely.

Vledder leaned forward.

"Did you know that van Ravenswood was the murderer, I mean before you pulled him out from underneath that table?"

DeKok nodded, then took the first careful sip from his glass.

"I knew," he said after he had fully enjoyed that first taste.

"How?"

DeKok took another sip and savored it. Then he placed his glass on the small table next to his chair.

"Because of a mistake."

"What mistake?"

"You see, the murderer placed Kruisberg's body almost in front of his son's door."

Vledder looked puzzled.

"Why was that a mistake? I thought it was a very cunning move. Young Kruisberg had said publicly he would kill his father. When the body was found near his house, suspicion had to fall immediately on him." Vledder looked intently at his mentor. "You yourself immediately assumed he was the perpetrator. Otherwise you would not have arrested him."

DeKok nodded guiltily.

"I assumed he was, you're right. Nevertheless it was a mistake on the part of the murderer—it put me on his trail."

Vledder shook his head.

"I don't understand."

DeKok spread both hands.

"Young Kruisberg had said publicly that he would kill his father, you're right about that. But to whom did he say it?"

"The people around him," said Vledder, who started to get a glimmer of the idea.

"Exactly. He told people around him, friends, family, and acquaintances. It was a relatively small circle." He raised a forefinger in the air. "And in that circle was the man, or the woman, who craftily took advantage of Ronny's threats. When I was finally convinced young Kruisberg had *not* killed his father, I knew where to look for the real murderer. The perpetrator had to be somebody from Ronny's circle of family and friends. I thought about the group and decided only one fit the bill…Robert Antoine van Ravenswood."

Vledder and the others looked at DeKok with admiration.

"Fantastic," whispered Fred Prins.

DeKok waved away the praise.

"The question was how to unmask him. How could I induce him to act? Then it came to me. I decided to use his own method. If Ronny's threats had reached the murderer, then I could feed the killer information in the same way, through Ronny."

Vledder looked wide-eyed and forgot to drink.

"The letter," he said softly. "The fake letter Kruisberg supposedly mailed to his son before he died."

DeKok picked up his glass and nodded. He took a long sip, draining the glass. Then he spoke again.

"Yes. The fake letter allegedly contained a list of names of people who had risen from the dead."

Appie Keizer moved closer.

"Is that Ravenswood guy suspected of more murders?" he wanted to know.

DeKok gave him a bitter smile.

"He committed a whole series of murders. It's up in the air whether we'll ever know the exact number."

Vledder looked pained.

"Truly, I still don't understand a thing. What was Assumburg's role? And what is the connection between van Ravenswood and the Holy Pact for the Dying?"

"He was the founder," said DeKok.

"What?"

"Yes, he bought an old building on Blood Mountain, in Antwerp," he added for Prins and Keizer. "Anyway," DeKok continued, "he called it Heaven's Gate. Using Brother Gregorius as the spiritual leader, he founded the Holy Pact of the Dying."

Vledder shook his head.

"I understood the founder was Paulus Verhoeven."

DeKok did not respond. Instead he lifted the bottle and poured another glass for everyone. After everybody's drink had been replenished, he replaced the almost empty bottle on the table and lifted his own glass. He took a long, satisfying swallow.

"I've been involved with crime for many years," he mused, studying the glass in his hand, "and each time I'm again amazed by the way in which a specific type of crime originates."

He placed the glass on the small table next to his chair and sat up a little straighter.

"Let's take Brother Gregorius, a man who described Paulus Verhoeven as a worthy, noble man. He said Verhoeven believed love for one's fellow man should not be a platitude and actions speak louder than words. Those words Brother Gregorius could have applied to himself, because Gregorius was sincerely concerned about the fate of his fellow human beings. He has tried several times to organize a homeless shelter, a haven for the outcasts of society. But each time he's had to abandon his plans for lack of funds."

Vledder wanted to say something, but DeKok motioned him to be silent.

"Then our brother," continued DeKok, "met Paulus Verhoeven, a man with a criminal background and a lively imagination. The meeting was not an accident. One might say both were laboring in the same vineyard. Verhoeven was known to have founded several so-called charitable organizations. He got people to collect or donate money so he could live the good life from their efforts. Verhoeven found the righteous Gregorius amusing. Over time, a sort of mutual appreciation developed. The result was that Verhoeven decided to support Brother Gregorius financially. When the homeless shelter in Kerkrade was no longer feasible, Verhoeven bought the old building on Blood Mountain for Brother Gre—"

"Yes, yes," said Vledder impatiently, "but you said that van Ravenswood was the founder in Antwerp."

"I'm coming to that," said DeKok patiently. He used the opportunity of the interruption to take another sip from his glass.

"Come on, then," urged Vledder.

"Very well," DeKok sighed. "Meanwhile the judicial police in Belgium were making life difficult for Verhoeven. There were all kinds of complaints against him stemming from his fraudulent sectarian activities. Convictions threatened. In his mind, Paulus saw the prison doors opening wide. It worried him."

"But—" began Vledder. DeKok shushed him and continued.

"One day, Verhoeven saw a man who looked a lot like him among the castaways who visited the temple. Verhoeven's criminal mind conceived what he thought to be a brilliant idea. He talked to the man, asked him about his family, inquired into the man's background. A criminal background or brush with the law could have resulted in the police having fingerprint records. Think about that for a moment. To make a long story short, Verhoeven invited the man for a vacation in Switzerland, in St. Moritz."

DeKok looked at Vledder.

"Now do you see the pattern?"

The young inspector nodded slowly.

"Yes, the derelict died."

DeKok took a deep breath.

"Indeed. Verhoeven pushed the unsuspecting man into a ravine...complete with his own identity papers. The unknown man was found several days later. He was buried under the name Paulus Verhoeven, permitting the real Paulus Verhoeven to return under the alias he liked so much, Robert Antoine van Ravenswood."

Mrs. DeKok entered the room carrying platters of culinary delights. Vledder, who knew the drill, hastily went to the kitchen to get the rest of the food. He placed the platters on the sideboard. Some of the platters were placed on warming plates. Then he returned to his seat, barely able to contain his impatience.

"What about Assumburg?" he asked.

DeKok did not answer but went to the sideboard, inviting the others to follow him. The men each took a plate and loaded it with the various hors d'oeuvres, canapés, and other finger foods Mrs. DeKok had prepared. DeKok, as usual, went heavily for the croquettes, but did not neglect the fresh steamed shrimp and satays. As the others returned to their seats with their heaping plates, DeKok poured a sherry for his wife. She took it with a fond smile and found a seat near the table.

When DeKok had reseated himself, he took a big bite of a croquette.

"Assumburg," said Vledder again.

"Give me a moment," said DeKok, with his mouth full.

Contentedly they all munched away under the benign smile of Mrs. DeKok, who sipped delicately from her glass of sherry.

"Hendrik-Jan Assumburg," said DeKok after a long interval, "is crooked. He's a con man, a grifter, and a swindler. He's also a completely untrustworthy rogue, a womanizer."

"Alright, but—" said Vledder.

"But," continued DeKok blandly, "let me first tell you about Ronald Kruisberg. After his flight, more than seven years ago, he wound up in Antwerp. Soon, though, he was destitute. He of course eventually found his way to Heaven's Gate. Brother Gregorius helped him and, after a while, gave him a regular position in the temple."

He stopped to eat the last of the shrimp and placed the empty plate on the low coffee table in front of him.

"Meanwhile Paulus Verhoeven," DeKok went on, "alias Robert Antoine van Ravenswood, discovered a hole in the market. There were, he discovered, a number of people for whom life had become extremely complicated. These people were prepared to pay handsomely to die. Well, our Paulus was an expert, so to speak, and 'took care of their deaths right to the grave.' Among the many destitute visitors to the temple he found many convenient candidates for violent deaths. Usually he arranged accidents, but with a twist. In all cases, identification of the body was either very difficult or downright impossible. All carried identification papers that survived in some form or another."

Mrs. DeKok shook her head, bewildered.

"How can anybody do such a thing?"

DeKok shrugged. In his long career he had seen so much crime that few things still surprised him.

"Assumburg," he continued, "also heard of the Holy Pact for the Dying. He had reached a point in his life in which dying appeared the only solution. He traveled to Antwerp and visited the temple."

"Now we're getting to him."

"I'm almost there," soothed DeKok. "Once van Ravenswood had made certain preparations, he traveled to St. Moritz with his intended victim. It was there Verhoeven had so successfully come back to life. But then, something happened that no one had foreseen…"

"What?" they all asked in chorus.

"Assumburg fell in love."

"Evelyn," said Vledder.

DeKok nodded.

"Assumburg, who had gotten to know Evelyn under his own name, suddenly didn't want to die anymore. Van Ravenswood, who also knew Evelyn, was furious. He could do little other than return to Antwerp with the intended victim."

DeKok paused and poured himself another glass of cognac. He held up the bottle to the others, but they all declined.

"I'll make coffee," said Mrs. DeKok and left the room.

DeKok took a long sip before he went on.

"Ronald Kruisberg, duly baptized as 'Brother Golgotha,' did not have his eyes in his pocket. He was aware of what was happening. And he, too, wanted to return home with a clean record. Although he lacked money, he managed to convince Brother Gregorius. He eventually emerged as Jan Vries."

DeKok drained his glass.

"Then, about two months ago, Assumburg invited van Ravenswood to come to Amsterdam. Assumburg's love had withered. He wanted to be rid of his new life with Evelyn. Van Ravenswood was initially reluctant to deal with Assumburg again. The affair in St. Moritz was still fresh in his mind. But when, against all expectations, he was himself mesmerized by Evelyn's charm, he decided to take on the job, but with one condition: Aunt Evelyn could not be left without being financially secure."

"Aha, I smell a rat," interjected Vledder.

"You're right. Assumburg agreed, but broke his word. He secretly took out heavy mortgages on his properties and mocked the funeral van Ravenswood had arranged by hiring a minister to *adorn* his eulogy. He then had the gall to take his entire balance out of Ijsselstein Bank the day after his funeral."

Appie Keizer grinned.

"A real rascal," he said mildly.

DeKok scratched the back of his head.

"'A man's word is his bond'…that disappeared a long time ago."

It sounded bitter.

Mrs. DeKok came back with a tray whereupon were cups, saucers, sugar, and cream.

"Shall I get the coffeepot?" asked Fred Prins.

"No, you sit there," she answered as she put the tray on the table.

Vledder just beat Appie on the way to the kitchen. He returned with the coffeepot.

All except DeKok poured themselves coffee. When DeKok's hand went back to the bottle, his wife placed a cup of coffee in his hand. He accepted it without protest.

After all were seated again, Vledder raised his hand for silence.

"Did van Ravenswood poison the men who were found in the water?" he asked.

DeKok shook his head.

"According to van Ravenswood, who made a complete confession this morning, it was Brother Gregorius. Van Ravenswood took care of the necessary mutilations."

"How did Gregorius get a hold of curarine?"

"He met a Dutch tramp, a former laboratory assistant who had stolen the stuff from his employer. In a tragic twist, the same lab assistant served as a substitute for Assumburg and was poisoned with the curarine he'd procured."

Mrs. DeKok looked shocked.

"As far as I know, you've never had such a sickening case before."

The gray sleuth smiled.

"My soul has not been sullied by it." He pointed at Vledder. "It seems best for you go to Antwerp tomorrow and give Chief Commissaris Opdenbroecke a complete report. My wife and I will pick you up at the station tomorrow night. I've taken a day off." He stole a glance at his wife. "I have to take her into town...to buy me a new suit."

The three of them walked across the Damrak after leaving Central Station.

"How did it go?" asked DeKok.

Vledder nodded with admiration.

"The judicial police made quick work. I was there when Brother Gregorius was arrested on Blood Mountain. It made me sad. There was a group of needy people waiting in front of the door, none of whom understood what was happening." He paused. "But with all that, we owe Brother Gregorius a lot of thanks."

"How's that?"

"He kept accurate records. There was a complete list of people van Ravenswood used as victims. Beside each name was the name of the *arisen* person, complete with real name and new alias."

DeKok pushed out his lower lip.

"That's going to stir the dust."

Vledder nodded.

"Opdenbroecke immediately used the information. Just before I left they came in with Rickie. They had picked him up in the bar of his hotel."

"Behind a *bolleke*."

Vledder laughed.

They entered the Victoria Hotel for a cup of coffee.

"What do you think about our adventures in Antwerp?" asked DeKok.

"Wonderful," said Vledder enthusiastically. "I've met nothing but nice people. Would you believe I even like

Brother Gregorius? If I weren't a Dutchmen, I'd want to be Flemish."

DeKok laughed out loud.

"What do you want? There are no better Dutchmen than the Flemish."

Mrs. DeKok gave her husband a disapproving look.

"Jurriaan," she said sternly, "don't let the Belgians hear you."

ABOUT THE AUTHOR

A. C. Baantjer is the most widely read author in the Netherlands. A former detective inspector of the Amsterdam police, his fictional characters reflect the depth and personality of individuals encountered during his nearly forty-year career in law enforcement.

Baantjer was honored with the first-ever Master Prize of the Society of Dutch-language Crime Writers. He was also recently knighted by the Dutch monarchy for his lifetime achievements.

The sixty crime novels featuring Inspector Detective DeKok written by Baantjer have achieved a large following among readers in the Netherlands. A television series based on these novels reaches an even wider Dutch audience. Launched nearly a decade ago, the 100th episode of the "Baantjer" series recently aired on Dutch channel RTL4.

In large part due to the popularity of the televised "Baantjer" series, sales of Baantjer's novels have increased significantly over the past several years. In 2001, the five millionth copy of his books was sold—a number never before reached by a Dutch author.

Known as the "Dutch Conan Doyle," Baantjer's following continues to grow and conquer new territory.

The DeKok series has been published in China, Russia, Korea, and throughout Europe. Speck Press is pleased to bring you clear and invigorating translations to the English language.

DeKok and the Geese of Death

Renowned Amsterdam mystery author Baantjer brings to life
Inspector DeKok in another stirring potboiler full of suspenseful
twists and unusual conclusions.
ISBN13: 978-0-9725776-6-3

DeKok and Murder by Melody

"Death is entitled to our respect," says Inspector DeKok, who finds
himself once again amidst dark dealings. A triple murder in the
Amsterdam Concert Gebouw has him unveiling the truth behind
two dead ex-junkies and their housekeeper.
ISBN13: 978-0-9725776-9-4

DeKok and the Death of a Clown

A high-stakes jewel theft and a dead clown blend into a single
riddle for Inspector DeKok to solve. The connection of the crimes
at first eludes him
ISBN13: 978-1-933108-03-2

DeKok and Variations on Murder

During one of her nightly rounds, housekeeper Mrs. van Hasbergen
finds a company president dead in his boardroom. She rushes up to
her apartment to call someone, but who? Deciding it better to return
to the boardroom, she finds the dead man gone.
ISBN13: 978-1-933108-04-9

DeKok and Murder by Installment

Although at first it seemed to be a case for the narcotics division,
this latest investigation soon evolves into a series of sinister murders involving drug smuggling and child prostitution
ISBN13: 978-1-933108-07-0

Boost

by Steve Brewer

Sam Hill steals cars. Not just any cars, but collectible cars, rare works of automotive artistry. Sam's a specialist, and he's made a good life for himself.

But things change after he steals a primo 1965 Thunderbird. In the trunk, Sam finds a corpse, a police informant with a bullet hole between his eyes. Somebody set Sam up. Played a trick on him. And Sam, a prankster himself, can't let it go. He must get his revenge with an even bigger practical joke, one that soon has gangsters gunning for him and police on his tail.

"…entertaining, amusing…. This tightly plotted crime novel packs in a lot of action as it briskly moves along."
—*Chicago Tribune*

"Brewer earns four stars for a clever plot, totally engaging characters, and a pay-back ending…."
—*Mystery Scene*

ISBN13: 978-1-933108-02-5

Killing Neptune's Daughter

by Randall Peffer

Returning to his hometown was something Billy Bagwell always dreaded. But he felt he owed it to Tina, the object of his childhood sexual obsession, to see her off properly. Even in death she could seduce him to her. Upon his return to Wood's Hole on Cape Cod, Billy's past with his old friends—especially his best friend, present-day Catholic priest Zal—floods his mind with classic machismo and rite-of-passage boyhood events. But some of their moments were a bit darker, and all seemed to revolve around or involve Tina...moments that Billy didn't want to remember.

This psycho-thriller carries Billy deeper and deeper into long-repressed memories of thirty-five-year-old crimes. As the days grow darker, Billy finds himself caught in a turbulent tide of past homoerotic encounters, lost innocence, rage, religion, and lust.

"...the perfect book for those who fancy the darker, grittier side of mystery. A hit-you-in-the-guts psychothriller, this is a compelling story of one man's search for truth and inner peace."
—*Mystery Scene*

ISBN13: 978-1-933108-05-6

speck

Nick Madrid Mysteries
by Peter Guttridge

No Laughing Matter

Tom Sharpe meets Raymond Chandler in this humorous
and brilliant debut. Meet Nick Madrid and the "Bitch of the
Broadsheets," Bridget Frost, as they trail a killer from Montreal to
Edinburgh to the ghastly lights of Hollywood.
ISBN13: 978-0-9725776-4-9

A Ghost of a Chance

New Age meets the Old Religion as Nick is bothered and
bewildered by pagans, satanists, and metaphysicians. Seances, sabbats,
a horse ride from hell, and a kickboxing zebra all come Nick's way
as he tracks a treasure once in the possession of Aleister Crowley.
ISBN13: 978-0-9725776-8-7

Two to Tango

On a trip down the Amazon, journalist Nick Madrid survives
kidnapping, piranhas, and urine-loving fish that lodge where a man
least wants one lodged. After those heroics, Nick joins up with a
Rock Against Drugs tour where he finds himself tracking down the
would-be killer of the tour's pain-in-the-posterior headliner.
ISBN13: 978-1-933108-00-1

The Once and Future Con

Avalon theme parks and medieval Excaliburger banquets are the last
things journalist Nick Madrid expects to find when he arrives at
what is supposedly the grave of the legendary King Arthur. As Nick
starts to dig around for an understanding, it isn't Arthurian relics, but
murder victims that he uncovers.
ISBN13: 978-1-933108-06-3

Peter Guttridge is the Royal Literary Fund Writing Fellow at Southampton University and teaches creative writing. Between 1998 and 2002 he was the director of the Brighton Literature Festival. As a freelance journalist he has written about literature, film, and comedy for a range of British newspapers and magazines. Since 1998 he has been the mystery reviewer for *The Observer*, one of Britain's most prestigious Sunday newspapers. He also writes about—and doggedly practices—astanga vinyasa yoga.

Praise for the Nick Madrid Mysteries

"Highly recommended."
—*Library Journal*, starred review

"…I couldn't put it down. This is classic Guttridge, with all the humor I've come to expect from the series. Nick is a treasure, and Bridget a good foil to his good nature."
—*Deadly Pleasures*

"Guttridge's series is among the funniest and sharpest in the genre, with a level of intelligence often lacking in better-known fare."
—*Baltimore Sun*

"…one of the most engaging novels of 2005. Highly entertaining…this is humor wonderfully combined with mystery."
—*Foreword*

"…Peter Guttridge is off to a rousing start…a serious contender in the mystery genre."
—*Chicago Tribune*

"[The] Nick Madrid mysteries are nothing if not addictively, insanely entertaining…but what's really important is the mix of good suspense, fast-and-furious one-liners and impeccable slapstick."
—*Ruminator*

"…both funny and clever. This is one of the funniest mysteries to come along in quite a while."
—*Mystery Scene*

For a complete catalog of our books please contact us at:

speck press

An imprint of Fulcrum Publishing
4690 Table Mountain Drive
Golden, Colorado 80403
e: books@speckpress.com
t: 800-992-2908
f: 800-726-7112
w: speckpress.com

Our books are available through your local bookseller.